P9-DMI-907

THE SIXTH SENSE

SECRETS FROM BEYOND

SURVIVOR

1

THE SIXTH SENSE

SECRETS FROM BEYOND

SURVIVOR

1

By David Benjamin

SCHOLASTIC INC.
New York   Toronto   London   Auckland   Sydney
Mexico City   New Delhi   Hong Kong

No part of this work may be reproduced, stored in a retrieval system, or transmitted in any form or by any means, electronic, mechanical, photocopying, recording, or otherwise, without written permission of the publisher. For information regarding permission, write to Scholastic Inc., Attention: Permissions Department, 555 Broadway, New York, NY 10012

ISBN 0-439-20270-1

Copyright © 2000 by Spyglass Entertainment Group, LP
All Rights Reserved. Used Under Authorization.

SCHOLASTIC and associated logos are trademarks and/or registered trademarks of Scholastic Inc.

12 11 10 9 8 7 6 5 4 3 2 1   0 1 2 3 4 5 6/0

Printed in the U.S.A.

First Scholastic printing, September 2000

For my mom and her mom
(for their mother sense)

Special thanks to Randi Reisfeld

THE SIXTH SENSE

SECRETS FROM BEYOND

SURVIVOR

1

ONE

They were after him.

Cole Sear knew he wasn't supposed to leave his teacher's sight. But the way he saw it, he didn't have any choice. The field trip had taken a turn that had nothing to do with the art hanging on the museum walls. Cole ducked from the back of the group and bolted from room to room, careful not to catch the eye of the guards.

They followed.

Cole knew he couldn't run forever. Eventually, they'd catch up to him. And he'd be caught.

So he swerved into a side room. Line drawings of bridges and buildings covered the wall. The light was dim. The room was empty.

For now . . .

Cole tried to hush his rapid breathing. He listened closely to the room outside. When he heard their voices — their voices coming closer — he ran out the opposite doorway.

He found himself in an octagonal room with a fountain in the center. A guard watched him closely. A few older people were sitting on benches, resting their feet. There were four doorways to choose from. Which one should he take?

He was frozen in decision.

And then it was too late.

He felt a hand on his shoulder.

"You're it!" one of the voices cried out.

It was his friend Jason. He'd been sitting between one of the older couples, waiting for Cole to arrive.

"You got me," Cole conceded. He saw the guard's hostile glance and knew what it meant. "We should probably get back to the group. Mr. Retlin might notice we're gone."

Jason nodded and waited for Cole to lead him back. Cole was surprised — happily surprised. He wasn't used to having people follow his lead. He wasn't really used to having friends, either.

The other kids in his class used to think he was a freak. They teased him, hounded him, and sometimes even threatened him — all because he could see things that they couldn't see. What Cole had wanted most in those days was to be ignored. He wanted to be invisible.

Invisibility had its advantages. He didn't have to worry about being stuffed into a locker. He didn't have to worry about being sent to the principal for making an observation the teacher couldn't handle. But invisibility also had its price. Cole didn't feel close to anyone at his school. There were some kids who had never teased him, who had never thought he was a freak. But as long as he was invisible, they couldn't see him. They ignored him like everybody else.

Someone — a man named Malcolm Crowe — had helped Cole realize he wasn't a freak, after all. Even though he had a gift to see things differently, he was still a normal kid. So Cole decided to make himself visible again. He was still scared of being taunted — but he was even more scared of going through life without having a friend. He didn't have to worry, though. Once he made himself visible, kids started to notice him. He found himself fitting in. School began to feel a little bit like a home.

Jason Black was now Cole's best friend, although Cole sometimes doubted that he was Jason's. Jason had a lot of best friends — a whole baseball team of best friends. But when Jason was with Cole, he felt he had all of Jason's attention. He wasn't used to such attention. He liked it.

He would even risk being in trouble, if it meant having fun with his friends. Which was exactly what he was doing now, ditching Mr. Retlin's art history tour to play tag in the Philadelphia Museum of Art with Jason and two other friends, Randi and Eduardo. If Mr. Retlin noticed they were gone, it wouldn't be a pretty sight. They had to get back as soon as possible.

Cole led Jason back to the room they'd originally left. The tour had already moved on. The two boys sped through the rooms, trying to find the rest of their classmates — Cole assumed that Randi and Eduardo had already made it back.

They passed another school group. Jason was starting to get nervous, saying that his mom would kill him if he got another detention from Mr. Retlin. Cole tried to calm him down — which was weird, because it was usually Jason who calmed *Cole* down.

Cole knew they didn't have time to look at the art, but when he got to one of the modern rooms, he had to stop. There were some glass boxes by a guy named Duchamp, one of them filled with sugar cubes. It was so incredibly weird that Cole was fascinated.

"Come on!" Jason urged.

Cole was about to plead for one more second. But his words were drowned out by another noise. A loud, buzzing noise coming from outside.

Cole darted to a nearby window to see what was going on. The noise was getting louder now — fiercer. An engine noise. A screaming noise.

The sound of the sky ripping. The sound of the world being torn apart.

And as Cole watched, an airplane came falling from the sky. It grazed over the roof of the museum — then plummeted into the park in front of it.

This can't be happening, Cole thought. He was stunned, paralyzed. Helpless.

The plane hit the ground. The explosion rocked the building with a deafening, blazing crash. The jet burst into pieces, fractured by an unseen hand. Flames and debris flew everywhere. A wing broke off and crashed into a nearby building. The sonic boom from the explosion pushed Cole back into Jason — all of the glass cases shook as the museum wobbled.

Cautiously, Cole moved back to the window. The heat of the flames pulsed against his face. Black smoke turned day into night. The sound of flames engulfed all voices, all sirens. Museum guards rushed down the steps, plunging themselves into danger to look for survivors.

Slowly, people emerged from the crash. Bleeding, burned, stumbling people. Crying, moaning, unaware of one another as they walked over smoldering metal and gasoline flames. There were dozens of them — over a hundred of them — pushing through the smoke, stumbling around the museum guards who ran right past them.

They spread out from the wreckage. Walking forward, not looking back. Headed to the city.

"Do you see them?" Cole whispered to Jason.

"See who?" Jason replied.

Cole felt a chill run through every cell of his body. The hairs on the back of his neck stood up. Jason was only confirming what he already knew:

All of these people were dead.

And they wouldn't leave until they were at peace.

TWO

The fire engines and the TV news vans arrived at the same time.

A museum guard spotted Cole and Jason by the window and pulled them away, ordering them to head directly to a big room at the back of the museum, where the school groups were gathering.

In all the confusion, Mr. Retlin hadn't noticed they were gone. He was relieved that they were here safely now, so he could call the school and say everyone was okay.

The smell of smoke was infiltrating the museum. Employees hastily set up fans and secured all the windows. Cole was worried that they were still in danger. The noise of the crash would not leave his ears. The ground still seemed to shake under his feet.

"Attention! May I have everyone's attention!"

A woman in a police uniform was standing at the front of the room. A hundred faces — most of them children's — turned to look at her.

"My name is Sergeant Nancy Mercado, and I'm from the Philadelphia Police Department," she said. "There are a few things I need to tell you. First, and most important, I want you to know that there is now a wall of fire engines between the crash site and this museum, so we do not believe you are in any danger. It's absolute chaos outside, and this is the safest place to be for now. If the situation changes, we will evacuate you immediately, and will need to you be calm and attentive."

As Sergeant Mercado spoke, the first of them entered the room. Out of the corner of his eye, Cole saw him. Cole had been able to see dead people for as long as he could remember, but it was still a surprise when they showed up like this. This one was a man, maybe Cole's mom's age, although it was hard to tell because his face and his clothes were burned badly. He put his hand against the wall and began to walk around the room. Cole watched his bleeding hand trail across the paintings on the wall without leaving a mark. The man didn't say a word. Only a broken moan escaped his lips.

Cole tried to keep his breathing normal. He didn't want anyone to see him scared. Not his friends. Not the dead person.

"If any of you saw the crash," Sergeant Mercado continued, "we're going to need to talk to you. We need to find out what caused it. Right now it's a mystery. It's possible something you saw might hold a clue to what happened. I want you to concentrate on remembering what happened. I'll need you to raise your hand so we can find out how to contact you."

Jason raised his hand high. Cole, a little more hesitant, followed.

A second person was now coming into the room. But instead of ignoring the crowd, she plunged into it — her body may have been dead, but her eyes were alive in fright.

"Warren?" she cried. "WARREN?"

Nobody but Cole heard her.

"Put your hands down!" Mr. Retlin ordered. He was glaring at Jason and Cole now. "What do you think this is, some kind of joke? There is no way you could have seen what happened from where we were. Put your hands down this instant."

Jason's hand dropped to his side. Cole could see the sergeant scanning the room and directing the eyewitnesses to a corner in the back of the room. There weren't that many people raising their hands, just an older girl from one of the other school groups, a few of the guards, and two women in Christmas sweaters.

Slowly Cole brought his hand back down. He didn't want to get himself and Jason into trouble. And he didn't really want to be asked what he'd seen. Because he could never tell the police the whole truth. They'd never believe him.

"Warren?" the woman was now sobbing, as the charred man made his second lap around the room. Another man walked in, his bones misaligned, his neck snapped. His head hung at an unnatural angle. But that didn't stop him from scanning the crowd. Something in his eyes made Cole shiver. This man was not distraught or disturbed.

No — he was angry.

He didn't say a word, just stared through the crowd.

Cole ducked behind Mr. Retlin.

"Is there anyone else?" Sergeant Mercado asked.

Cole could feel the broken man's gaze moving in his direction. For the first time since Malcolm Crowe had left, Cole felt true fear.

"Over here!" a man cried. Cole looked — it was the guard who had pulled him and Jason from the window. Now he was pointing right at them. "These two saw it."

Mr. Retlin wouldn't believe it. "They were with me!" he insisted.

"No, we weren't," Jason mumbled.

Mr. Retlin swung around to confront Cole.

"Is this true?" he asked.

But Cole wasn't paying attention anymore. He was looking at the man with the broken neck — who was staring right at him.

"Is it?" Mr. Retlin's face was now growing red.

Sergeant Mercado was over with them now. "It's okay," she said gently. "It's okay if we're all just a little afraid. Why don't the two of you come with me for a second, so we can get your information."

As Cole and Jason walked over to the other eyewitnesses, the broken man's gaze followed them. Cole didn't even have to look to know this. He felt it. He tried to put as many people as possible between them, but that did no good. The man knew where he was.

The eyewitnesses made a small circle at the edge of the large crowd. Cole couldn't see the girl who'd raised her hand.

"As soon as you can," Sergeant Mercado said after all their addresses had been taken, "I need you to write down every single thing you saw. I don't care how little it is — little facts can solve big mysteries. We'll be contacting you soon for interviews; right now, I have to head back outside. Thank you all — I know this isn't easy, but it could be a big help."

The eyewitnesses headed back to their groups. Jason was already walking back to Mr. Retlin when Cole felt a hand on his shoulder.

He turned to see the high-school girl who'd raised her hand. Her hair was blond. Her face was pale.

Her dark turtleneck was covered in blood.

"I need your help," she whispered.

"Not now," Cole murmured, shivering. He could see Jason turning back to look at him. Mr. Retlin looking at him.

The broken-necked man still looking at him.

"I understand," the girl said. "I'll see you later."

Without another word, she was gone.

THREE

As the bus finally took them away from the museum, Cole could see the dead people wandering alone through the streets. Some turned as the bus drove past them — they could sense him as strongly as he could sense them. Cole ducked down in his seat and prayed they would not see him. He didn't look out the window again until the bus was safely back at school.

Cole's mom couldn't speak for a minute or two, she was crying so hard. They were tears of relief.

The two of them were sitting in their car in front of his school. Just pausing for a second before driving on. Cole knew his mom was a little more emotional than most moms. But this time, he saw that a

13

lot of the other kids' cars weren't moving, either. Not yet.

"I was just so worried," Lynn Sear said, squeezing Cole's hand. "When I heard on the news that a jet had crashed at the museum — oh, my God, honey, I thought the worst. I called the museum and no one answered. I called the school and they didn't know anything. So I just sat there watching the TV. Then the school secretary called and she was like an angel. She told me everyone was okay. And I just lost it, Cole. I completely lost it. Then suddenly it was all right."

She turned the key in the ignition and started to drive. Cole could tell she had questions for him, but she was afraid he wasn't ready to answer them yet.

"I'm okay," he reassured her.

His mom nodded. "You didn't see any of it, did you?"

Cole was tempted to lie. It would make things so much easier if he said no — his mom wouldn't have any reason to worry.

But saying no wouldn't be honest. And Cole and his mom had vowed to be honest with each other, no matter what. She was the only person alive who knew his biggest secret.

"I did see it, Mom," Cole said quietly. "I saw the crash."

Lynn kept driving, stealing glances over at Cole when not looking at the road.

Cole remembered the crash and tried not to shiver. "It was so strange. Like a movie, only I knew it was real. I could feel it."

"Oh, honey . . ."

"I saw them, Mom," Cole continued, afraid that if he stopped now he'd never start again. "There were so many of them."

Lynn stared straight at the road. "Dead?" she asked.

"Yes."

They were parking in front of their house now. But Cole's mom made no move to leave the car.

"Honey," she said carefully, looking Cole right in the eye, "I'm not sure I know how to help you here. You know I believe you. I'm sure you *did* see them. But I don't want it to get to you. We're doing so well right now. *You're* doing so well. I don't want this to affect that."

"It won't, Mom," Cole promised her.

"I hope not." Lynn leaned in to give Cole another hug. He accepted it gladly.

The house was quiet when Cole entered.

Now it was his turn to be relieved.

While Lynn went to fix dinner, Cole turned on the television. Live reporters and studio experts appeared on every local channel, all saying the same thing under red banners that proclaimed THE CRASH OF FLIGHT 333.

"The big question tonight is what caused this bizarre crash in downtown Philadelphia. Was it a technical malfunction, pilot error, terrorist attack, or the result of a freak weather condition? Right now, nobody knows. The investigation has only just begun. . . ."

The cameras focused on the burning wreckage. The pictures were so flat compared to what Cole had seen. They felt so distant.

Cole wanted to believe he wasn't a part of this story. He wanted to believe that there was no way he could help.

But what if he *had* seen something? What if he could find out why the plane had gone down?

He couldn't, right? Cole tried to convince himself of that. He was just a kid. There would be hundreds of police officers and investigators on the case. There would be hundreds of witnesses from all the buildings around the art museum. No way had he seen anything they hadn't also seen.

Except the dead people . . .

On the TV, the police chief said there were many cops and firefighters on the scene. It had been confirmed that a number of bystanders had been killed along with the people on the plane. As the police chief was about to answer the reporter's next question, she held her hand to her earpiece and asked him to stop for a second. She and the chief hung in silence for a moment as she listened. Then she looked straight into the camera and said, "We now have unconfirmed reports that there is a survivor. I repeat, a survivor has been found!"

The police chief quickly exited off camera to check this latest development. Cole watched, transfixed, as the story played out. There was, indeed, a survivor — an eight-year-old girl who had been pulled from the wreckage.

Soon Cole's mom was beside him, watching quietly. Once the news started to repeat itself, they went into the kitchen for dinner. They didn't turn off the TV. Like the rest of the world, they wanted more news — more survivors, more hope.

But by the end of the evening, only the one survivor held on, in a coma at a local hospital.

"Pray for her," Lynn said before they went to sleep.

Cole already had.

FOUR

That night, the visits began.

Cole had been so exhausted by the day's events that he'd gone to sleep easily.

Waking up was harder.

He'd pulled blanket after blanket onto his bed. He'd been so cold. He wanted to believe that the radiators weren't working. But when he woke up, he knew.

It was cold because the dead people had found him.

Cole shot out of bed, instantly aware.

He looked over to his desk and saw the girl from the museum watching him, her pale skin and blond hair glowing vaguely in the nighttime light.

"I was waiting for you to wake up," she said.

Cole couldn't deal with this. Her eyes were kind; instinctively, he knew she did not mean him any harm. Still, she was in his house. *In his room.*

Quickly, he pulled one of the blankets around his body and stumbled out of his room. He heard other sounds within the house — terrifying sounds.

The girl was not the only one here.

Cole moved forward. The hall light had been turned off. The hallway was tomb-dark.

Cole struggled to see in the darkness. He heard garbled words and the hitting of a wall.

At the end of the hallway, the kitchen light went on. The brightness creeped out from the bottom of the doorway.

"Mom?" he called out quietly.

There was no answer.

"Mom?" he asked again. But this time, he knew.

It wasn't her.

It was so cold.

With a shaking hand, Cole pushed open the kitchen door.

He was momentarily blinded by the full force of the light. Then he saw a man sitting at the kitchen table, an empty bowl in front of him. One of his ears had been burned off, but his suit had remained intact. He looked young underneath his wounds — in his twenties maybe.

"It's all my fault," he told the bowl. Then he looked up at Cole and said the same thing.

Cole pushed back through the doorway, his heart pounding. He had to get away. He ducked into the living room, where the woman was now crying for Warren, looking out the window as if he'd appear at any moment.

Cole pressed himself against the wall and watched. He prayed she would not see him.

There were three dead people. In his house.

He heard a crash from the laundry room.

Four.

Cole had to check it out. He had to know who was here.

Another crash — clothes and hangers falling to the floor. The burned man from the museum — the one who'd trailed his hand across the paintings — was flailing through the laundry, absentmindedly tearing a shirt.

"Stop that!" Cole cried desperately. "Leave us alone!"

He hoped his mom was still asleep. He hoped she was safe.

The man began to put the shirt on, over his char-black clothes.

Cole ran back to his room. The girl hadn't moved.

"What do you want?" he asked. He tried to sound

calm. He knew that if he gave the dead people what they wanted, they usually went away.

"I need you to help her," she answered.

"Who?"

"My sister."

"Where is she?"

"In the hospital."

Cole heard a noise on the other side of the door. Another dead person. Coming closer.

"What are you looking at?" the dead girl asked. She couldn't be more than a year older than Cole.

"Nothing." Cole knew that dead people never saw or heard one another.

"What's your name?"

Cole had never been asked this question by a dead person before. He didn't see any harm in answering honestly.

"I'm Cole," he said.

"I'm Marisa. Will you help me?"

Cole nodded.

"I'll let you get back to sleep, then."

Something about Marisa's voice let Cole know he was safe with her. She didn't seemed consumed by anger or despair like most of the others.

Outside his room, he heard the woman call for Warren again. But otherwise the night had turned quiet. Except for the sound of his racing, scared heart. The dead people hadn't gone away — there was no way to make them go away — but it was possible they wouldn't disturb him for a few hours.

"Don't worry," Marisa said. "Please rest."

He got back into bed and closed his eyes. He thought Marisa would leave him alone until morning. But just as he was about to slip away into dreaming, he heard her voice again, trembling for the first time.

"Cole," she said, "I know I'm dead."

Then he heard the sounds of her leaving the room, leaving him to sleep.

"Cole, they were here, weren't they?"

Cole woke up to find his mother in the doorway, looking tired and sad. She was holding a shredded blouse in her hands.

She came over and sat on his bed.

"Look at my face," she said. "I need to know. You didn't do this, did you?"

"No," Cole quietly answered.

"Did you see who did?"

Cole nodded. "A man from the plane."

"Thank you." Lynn stood up from the bed and left the room.

Cole felt bad — he hated for his mom to be dragged into these things. And at the same time, he was secretly glad, because before he had been all alone, desperately searching for false explanations for all of the things the dead people had done. Now he didn't have to lie to his mom anymore. Instead, they had to deal with the truth, which was sometimes just as hard.

Lynn didn't say another word to Cole about the nighttime visitors. They had breakfast like a normal family. Neither Cole nor Lynn turned on the radio or the TV. They would live a few minutes without the outside world. They wanted to focus inside. They wanted to imagine a world where it was calm and peaceful, even if they were pretending.

Cole ate his cereal and then headed for the shower. The events of last night had left him tired and sluggish. He'd have to hustle if he wanted to make it to school on time.

In the shower, he made promises to himself. He wouldn't let the visitors affect his life. He wouldn't acknowledge them if they showed up in school. He wouldn't let them interfere with his friendships and his schoolwork — he wouldn't let them turn him into a freak again. It was true that he'd never had to deal with more than a few dead people at a time before. But he swore to himself that he could handle it. He would have to handle it. He would have to be in control.

Cole turned off the water and reached for a towel. Already he felt better. He was ready to face the day.

He pulled back the shower curtain and found the broken-necked man standing there, waiting for him.

Cole screamed and fell back, pulling the shower curtain down with him.

"*Skazhi im, chto ya etogo ne delal!*" the man yelled, lunging forward.

Cole curled tight and prepared himself for the punches. For the pain.

The door flew open.

Cole looked up and saw the broken-necked man was gone. Cole's mom was there instead.

"Are you okay?" she asked. "What happened?"

He'd pulled the shower curtain completely off the rod. It draped over him as he stood up in the tub.

"It was them, wasn't it?" Lynn asked fiercely.

Cole didn't have to answer. His mom was already spinning around, as if she could see them.

"STAY AWAY FROM MY SON!" she yelled. "I swear to God, STAY AWAY FROM HIM!"

This was the worst part for Cole, knowing that he and his mom felt the same pain — the kind that comes from knowing there's nothing you can do.

There was no way to keep them away.

FIVE

Cole didn't know news could travel so fast, but it was clear to him from the moment he walked through the door that he and Jason were the new celebrities at his school. The other kids were giving him more respect than they ever had before — all because he'd looked out a window and seen a plane crash. Even Tommy Tamasino, formerly the school's biggest celebrity because of his acting in cheezy TV commercials, shot Cole a glance that verged on awe.

Jason was in the center of the hallway, surrounded by at least a dozen other students.

"So then there was this big fireball," he was describing. "The whole sky was fire. The plane just exploded in front of my eyes."

"Cool!" one kid exclaimed.

"*Really* cool," another echoed.

Cole wanted to walk past. He didn't think it was cool at all. Nobody — not even Jason — got that people had *died* in that explosion. They were treating it like some fireworks display.

"Hey, Cole," Jason called out. The crowd parted to let him through.

Cole had no choice. Now that he had friends, he couldn't just walk away from them.

"Hey, Jason," he responded. Luckily, the second bell rang. The crowd began to disperse.

"Pretty crazy, huh?" Jason asked. "I was up all night watching the news. When my parents told me to go to sleep, I told them I was having nightmares. How about you? Sleep much?"

"Kind of, I guess." Cole couldn't think of anything else to say. It never occurred to him to tell the truth.

There was a special meeting for Mr. Retlin's class as soon as school started, even though they didn't usually have Mr. Retlin until fourth period. One of the school's guidance counselors — someone who Cole didn't like much, due to their constant run-ins during his "freak" phase — said that she was available to talk to anyone who was experiencing any difficulties due to the "unfortunate accident." The principal commended them and Mr. Retlin for sticking together yesterday. He also mentioned that investigators might be coming to the school to ask them questions, and the students were to show them full cooperation.

Cole walked warily through the halls between classes, waiting for one of the dead people to show up. The living people were hard enough to deal with, wanting details ("So did you see any flying body parts?") or sharing confidences ("My aunt died in a plane crash — it was awful."). Even the teachers were looking at him a little strangely; he was their connection to headline news. In class, he found it hard to concentrate. For some reason he found himself writing "Skazhi im, chto ya etogo ne delal!" over and over in his notebook, and then on the back of his hand. What could that mean?

Someone was waiting for him after Mr. Retlin's fourth-period class — a tall African-American man wearing a gray suit and a gray hat. As Cole left the classroom, the man called out his name and flashed a badge.

"Are you Cole Sear?" the man asked.

"Yes."

"Would you mind coming with me? I'm Detective

James Brown. No relation to the other James Brown." He waited a beat, then laughed. "You don't know who I'm talking about, do you?"

"He's . . . a singer?" Cole offered.

Detective James Brown seemed pleased. "Very good. Let's head to the guidance office — I've set up a little office there."

They went to Ms. Holmes's office, since she was away on maternity leave. The guidance secretary didn't even look up as they went inside.

Detective Brown sat down at the desk. He didn't remove his hat. He gestured for Cole to sit down across from him.

"I just have a few questions," he began. "I'm going to be honest with you, and I'm hoping you will be honest with me. Some crash investigations are open-and-shut cases. But most take ages to get through. There's a load of evidence, and very little of it really counts. But you have to gather as much information as possible, because you never know which piece is going to solve the puzzle.

"Now, I was actually on the ground, right by the museum when the crash occurred. So I already have *my* version of what happened. I need to hear yours, and your friend Jason's. That will help the police's investigation."

Detective Brown set up a tape recorder on the

desk. Cole heard something behind him . . . and felt a prickling of cold. He turned to find Marisa there, waiting.

"Cole?" Detective Brown asked. Cole turned back, and saw that the policeman had noticed his distraction. His hands began to shake a little. He gripped his armrest so the detective wouldn't see.

For the next ten minutes, Cole told what he'd seen. Every detail seemed important to the detective. Cole wasn't sure whether he was helping, or whether nothing he'd seen really mattered.

Detective Brown kept asking the same question. "Are you sure the plane didn't explode until it hit the ground?"

Cole knew why the detective was asking this — they had to determine whether it was the crash, or maybe a bomb, that had caused the explosion.

Cole was pretty sure it hadn't been a bomb. He was pretty sure the plane hadn't exploded before it hit the ground.

The tape recorder clicked off. Detective Brown patted his pockets, then scowled.

"Forgot to bring an extra tape," he said. "Maybe they have one outside. I'll be back."

The detective left the room . . . leaving Cole alone with Marisa.

"We have to go soon," she said. "I just came from the hospital. You must go and see her."

The hospital.

"Is your sister the survivor?" Cole asked.

Marisa nodded. "She's in danger."

"But what can I do?"

Before Marisa could answer, Detective Brown came back into the room — without a new tape. There was nothing to stop Marisa from continuing to speak. After all, Detective Brown couldn't hear her. The only reason for her to stop was so Cole wouldn't get into trouble.

She knew it — and was doing it for him.

"What did you say?" Detective Brown asked, looking frustratedly at the tape recorder he could no longer use. "Did you say something as I was coming in?"

"Just talking to myself," Cole said. This was usually his excuse. He was surprised at how easily people accepted it.

Detective Brown looked at him curiously for a second, then clearly decided not to pursue the subject . . . yet.

"I guess that's all for now," he said. "I'll be in touch if I think of anything else. I'll also give you my number, if you want to get a hold of me."

Cole shook the man's hand and headed back to class. As he was leaving, Ms. Keller, the guidance counselor who'd talked to his class earlier in the day, walked in and asked him if he'd come to see her. Cole told her he'd been in to talk to a detective.

"Oh, are the police here already?" she asked. Then she headed inside to check.

Cole left before she could ask any more questions.

Marisa followed him to lunch. She didn't say a word. She didn't have to — Cole knew what she wanted.

He headed to his locker. Hiding himself behind the locker door, he told her he couldn't leave school until the end of the day — if he disappeared, especially today, people would notice and he'd get into trouble.

Marisa nodded. But she didn't look pleased.

He prayed she wouldn't get angry.

She faded back as he entered the lunchroom. Jason waved him over; they usually sat together.

"What a crazy day!" Jason said, devouring a bag of potato chips.

"Did you talk to Detective Brown?" Cole asked.

"Who?"

"The detective. From the police department."

"Nope. Mr. Retlin told me the investigators wouldn't be here until the afternoon."

Cole was confused, but he tried not to show it.

He was even more confused later that afternoon, when the investigators *did* show up. There were two of them, from the Federal Aviation Agency.

"We are the government bureau that investigates crashes," one of the investigators, Agent McCrum, explained.

"So it would be a big help if you could tell us what you saw," the other investigator, Agent Masino, added.

"Are you working with Detective Brown?" Cole asked.

The agents shared a blank look.

"He talked to me this morning," Cole added.

"Must be one of the local cops," Agent Masino mumbled to Agent McCrum. "Interfering, no doubt."

"This is *our* case now," Agent McCrum assured Cole, "although of course we'll be working closely with the Philadelphia Police. There must have been some sort of mix-up this morning — I hope you won't mind telling me and Agent Masino again about what you saw."

Cole could see he was in for a long afternoon.

And Marisa was waiting for him outside.

SIX

"Let's go," she said as soon as school was over.

Cole couldn't think of another excuse. He knew his mom wouldn't be home until six-thirty, when her job was done. He knew he had to help Marisa.

They took the bus to the hospital. Cole showed his pass to get on. Marisa just walked right on. She knew she didn't have to pay.

She knew she was dead.

Cole was surprised by this — most dead people didn't know they were dead. Instead, they wandered the world without realizing they had no effect. They were in denial, and the denial colored their every action and thought. Cole knew he had to be very careful around these dead people — if he let them know they were dead, awful things could happen. Suddenly their denial would be gone, and all that would be left was anger and pain.

The bus was nearly empty. Marisa could sit beside Cole. They could talk without anyone noticing.

"Thank you for doing this," Marisa said.

"Can I ask you something?" Cole was amazed at how much older she seemed. Even though she was high-school age, she talked like an adult. Had death taught her that, or was she like that before she died? There was no way for Cole to know.

"What do you want to know?"

"How did you find me?"

Marisa shook her head. "I don't know. I walked into the museum . . . after the crash. I still didn't know what was going on. I found that room where you all were — it was like something was drawing me there. I stood in the back and listened to the policewoman talk. I raised my hand and saw you looking at me. I still thought I was alive then, although I didn't know what was going on. Then I realized that no one else was seeing me. Only you. I realized what had happened. And I wasn't surprised."

"Why not?"

"I wish I knew. As the plane was going down — I can't really remember it now, but maybe *as* it was going down, I knew I was going to die. So I was prepared. When I was actually dead, it wasn't so much of a surprise.

"As soon as I realized, I walked back to the wreckage. I walked right over to where Emily was, and I knew she was still alive. But there was nothing I could do. I saw the rescuers getting closer. So I headed back into the museum — headed back to you. I needed your help, but I knew you couldn't — not then. So I went back out and eventually managed to save my sister. I created a disturbance so the searchers could find her."

"So why do you need me now, if she's saved?"

"Because there's still a threat. I don't know why. But somehow I know — she's in danger. I won't be able to move on until she's safe."

"Do you want to move on?" Cole asked.

For the first time, Marisa smiled. But it was a sad smile.

"No," she said. "I want to stay. But I know I can't. The only way for me to stay is for Emily to be in trouble. And I don't want that."

There was complete chaos outside the hospital. Reporters and TV crews from around the world surrounded the building, awaiting an update on the survivor.

"I've found a back way," Marisa told Cole, leading him forward. Only one person made him slow down — alongside the hospital was a man in smoke-black rags, his torn skin hanging in loose clumps. No one was paying attention to him.

"Felicia?" he mumbled. "Felicia!"

"Can you see him?" Cole asked Marisa.

"See who?"

Cole pointed, but Marisa couldn't see. Like all the ghosts Cole had known before, Marisa couldn't see other dead people. Cole hurried on before the man noticed him. He noted the name: Felicia.

The inside of the hospital was much calmer than the outside, with the doctors and nurses going on as if the media circus didn't exist.

"You're going to have to be careful," Marisa warned. "Be sure to look like you know where you're going. Latch onto adults if you can. If anyone asks, tell them you're one of Emily's friends from Allentown. A few of her friends are supposed to visit, so you can just say you came early."

Cole followed Marisa through the maze of stark-white corridors. It was very, very quiet — all the pain and sorrow kept behind closed doors.

Marisa led him to Emily's room. A number of times he had to duck past nurses' stations and camouflage himself with a pair of adults who could pass as his parents. Still, he was surprised that nobody stopped him. They clearly had more important things on their minds.

Marisa wouldn't go into the room with Cole.

"I'll wait here," she said. "I can't see her right now. It hurts too much."

"But what do you want me to do?" Cole asked.

"I'm not sure. But I know you can help."

Warily, Cole stepped inside the room. He heard the beeps and the whirs first — all of the instruments keeping Emily alive, charting their own progress. Then he saw Emily, so small in the bed. She had been burned badly, but not beyond recognition. You could still tell she was an eight-year-old girl, with dark hair and wide eyes. Her breathing was shallow, her expression impassive. She looked on the border of life and death.

A woman stood at Emily's side, holding her hand. They were opposites of each other — as red and swollen as Emily's skin was, the woman was pale and smooth; as expressionless as Emily's face was, the woman's was etched in sorrow. They were opposites . . . and yet Cole could see the bond between them. Anyone could tell they were family.

The woman looked up from Emily as Cole entered.

"Can I help you?" she asked.

"I'm a friend of Emily's," Cole lied.

"Oh?" the woman studied Cole carefully. "I'm Emily's mother. Have we met before? Wait — are you Thomas? Of course you are!"

Cole nodded. He hated lying, but he couldn't see any way around it.

"Well, how nice of you to come. I'm sure Emily . . ." She couldn't finish the sentence. She'd begun to cry.

"I'm sorry," she sniffed. "They keep telling me I need my rest. But I can't leave her. I haven't seen her father for years — I don't even know if he knows — and her sister is . . . oh, God. I can't even think of it. I can't think of anything except getting Emily better."

Cole looked at Emily, unconscious in her bed. Did she dream? Did she know what had happened?

Was there anything he could do?

Emily's mother had fallen into silence now. They both watched as the machines kept Emily alive.

The door opened. A nurse walked in.

"What are you doing here?"

"He's a friend of Emily's," her mother explained.

Cole was hoping he wouldn't have to explain any further. But before he could find out, another person entered the room.

A dead person.

The broken-necked man.

He looked angry now. Furious. Something had happened. Cole had no idea what. He could feel his blood turning to ice.

"Skazhi im, chto ya etogo ne delal!" the man yelled.

The nurse didn't flinch. The nurse didn't hear.

"Are you sure you should be here?" she asked.

Cole pushed for the doorway.

He had to get away.

Now.

"Skazhi im, chto ya etogo ne delal!"

The man followed him into the hall.

"Cole?" Marisa asked. But Cole couldn't stop. He looked back and saw the man coming after him.

He ran down the hallway. Orderlies yelled at him to slow down.

The man wouldn't let him go. He kept screaming, enraged.

What had Cole done?

He had to get away. He ran around a corner, not looking where he was going. He ran right into some-one —

Right into Detective Brown.

"Hey, what's the hurry?" the detective demanded. "And what are you doing here?"

Cole looked back. His pursuer was hanging back. Waiting.

"Cole," Detective Brown said abruptly. "What is it?"

Cole sputtered an explanation about visiting a relative in the hospital. Detective Brown wasn't buying it, but he wasn't going to make a scene in the middle of the hospital, either. He looked down at Cole's hands — Cole couldn't understand why, until he looked down. There, written in blue ink, were his scribblings — *Skazhi im, chto ya etogo ne delal!*

"What's that?" Detective Brown asked, tipping his hat up a little for a closer look.

"Nothing," Cole said, putting his hand in his pocket.

"Cole, why do I think you're not telling me everything?"

Cole knew he had to look the cop in the eye. "I told you everything. And then I told Agents McCrum and Masino everything."

"Oh, so they saw you, too, did they?" Detective Brown whistled. "Guess they feel they can't trust the locals. I'll tell you something, though, Cole — I might not be a part of their investigation, but I'm not off the case. Because I was there — right there — and I want answers as much as anybody else. If you know something that I don't, I'm going to find it out. So don't be withholding from me."

"Yes, sir," Cole mumbled, trying to keep the tension out of his voice. If Detective Brown only knew what the truth would mean.

"I was going to head out soon. Do you need a ride?"

"No," Cole said. "Someone's waiting for me outside."

The detective nodded curtly and said, "We'll be in touch."

It was much easier for Cole to leave the hospital than it was to get in. He didn't have to take any back way.

"Did you see her?" Marisa asked once he'd found her.

Cole nodded.

"Can you help?"

Cole told her the truth —

He wasn't sure.

SEVEN

When Cole got home, the living room was trashed — the furniture upturned, the television blaring. Nothing was in its right place.

His house was no longer his.

"Oh, my God," Marisa gasped. She could see the damage. But she couldn't see that the damagers were still in the room.

The burned man was crawling on the ground, running his hands over the floor. The distraught woman had moved to a new window, crying for Warren.

Cole walked over to her. There was at least one thing he *thought* he could put right.

"Felicia?" he said softly. She didn't respond.

He repeated it. "Felicia?"

She turned to him and snapped, "I'm not Felicia. I'm Gwen. Where's Warren? What have you done with Warren?"

She was attacking him now. Pushing him.

"I don't know," he said, trying to get away as the cold chill of fear gripped him.

She gave up. "Then what good are you?" she spat. Then she returned to the window, waiting.

Cole knew he had to clean up before his mother got home. If she saw this mess, she'd flip out — for all the right reasons. Cole wanted to cry out; he didn't want to go through this all over again. The tearing apart of his house. The opened drawers. The jagged rips in the furniture and his clothes. The constant threat. The never-ending noise.

If they could see him, why couldn't they see what they were doing to him?

Why couldn't they care?

Only Marisa seemed to understand. The rest of them would continue to shred up his life until they got what they wanted. And he would have to clean up the mess.

He headed to the broom closet and opened it up. Just then, a hand reached out — and pulled him inside, slamming the door behind him.

Cole felt the ice shooting through him. In a

panic, he banged at the door — but it wouldn't budge. He screamed, but nobody would hear.

"It's all my fault," the young man with the burned-off ear hissed, gripping Cole's arm tight enough to leave a mark.

"What is?" Cole desperately tried to wrangle out of his grasp.

"I hurt them."

"Who?"

"It's all my fault."

The dead man wouldn't let him go. And he wouldn't say any more. Just, "It's all my fault." Over and over again.

Cole pushed and clawed. Finally, the man grew tired. He fell to the back of the closet and loosened his grip. Cole pulled free and yanked open the door. Then he slammed it back behind him, leaning heavily and breathing deeply.

It was happening again. He couldn't control it. All his fear was returning.

He was shutting down.

It was just like before — before Malcolm had come and showed Cole what he had to do — that the dead people needed him to listen to them. Now there was too much to listen to. There were too many of them. They were all closing in.

By the time Cole's mom returned home, he'd cleaned up so she didn't notice anything wrong.

"Ask me how my day was," she said, giving Cole a kiss and throwing her keys on the side table.

"How was your day?" Cole asked dutifully.

"Well, let's see." Lynn kicked off her shoes. "I discovered this pill that would make me feel fully rested on only three hours of sleep. So I gave up coffee, felt wonderfully awake, got a massage, and took on a third job as a travel writer. We're leaving for Maui tomorrow. And how was *your* day?"

Cole paused. Some days his mom played this game to cheer him up; today he had to play it to show her he didn't *need* cheering up.

"Well," he said, forcing a smile, "I got into college today. Early, early acceptance. But I told Harvard I wanted to finish sixth grade first."

"That seems right to me," Lynn said with mock seriousness. "Should we celebrate with some pizza?"

Cole pretended enthusiasm. He was glad to see there weren't any dead people in the kitchen.

Lynn went to turn up the thermostat. When she got back, she asked Cole if he'd heard the news.

Cole shook his head.

"They've found the black box," Lynn reported, taking some pizza dough from the refrigerator. "You know — the flight recorder. It will tell them everything that happened in the cockpit, and all the technical details. So hopefully they'll find out what happened. Oh — and that little girl is still in a coma. Her poor family . . ."

Cole didn't tell his mom about his visit to Emily; instead he told her about the investigators and the questions they'd asked.

Lynn poured sauce on the pizza, then added cheese and garlic.

"Did you tell them about — you know?"

The dead people.

"No," Cole answered. "I don't think that would help."

Lynn nodded. "You're right. Let's not ask for trouble."

After the pizza was in the oven, Cole's mom headed to her room to change. Cole stayed in the kitchen and took out his homework. Marisa walked in soon after. She looked into the oven, sat down across from Cole, and started to cry.

"What is it?" Cole asked gently.

From the way she was sitting, he couldn't really see the bloodstains on her clothes. She looked almost normal, almost alive.

"The pizza," she said, wiping away her tears. "It's so silly, but we used to have pizza all the time.

My mother would make it, just like that. And now . . . now I can't even smell it. Can you smell it?"

Cole inhaled. And there it was — the aroma of garlic, tomatoes, and the slight tinge of baking bread.

"I don't think I could even taste it if I tried," Marisa continued.

"Could you maybe remember the taste?" Cole suggested.

"I can try, but I'll still miss it."

Lynn was in the doorway, watching Cole and his side of the conversation.

Marisa stayed at the table as Lynn took the pizza out of the oven. Cole watched her trying to smell.

"Who is she?" Cole's mom asked.

Cole was surprised. Usually his mom tried to ignore the dead people's presence.

"Her name is Marisa," he said. "How did you know it was a girl?"

"From your voice. Does she . . . ?"

"She knows she's dead."

"And she's here right now?"

Cole looked at Marisa, who nodded.

"Uh-huh."

"How old is she?"

"Fifteen," Marisa said.

"Fifteen," Cole repeated, so Lynn could hear.

Lynn leaned against the kitchen counter, the pizza cooling behind her. Cole could tell she was trying — trying not to cry, trying to believe.

"Is she the one who wrecked the house?" she asked.

Cole guessed he hadn't done such a great job cleaning up after all.

"No. That was someone else."

"Is that one here now?"

"No."

"What does she want?"

Cole hesitated, but Marisa said, "Tell her. Let her help you."

"Her sister is the one in the coma."

"I see."

"She needs help."

"I see."

Lynn paused for a moment, holding her hand to her mouth, thinking hard.

"I can't believe I'm saying this, but would you mind asking her to leave the room? I want to talk to you alone."

Marisa was already out of her chair.

"She can hear you, Mom," Cole explained. "She's leaving now." When Marisa was gone, he added, "It's okay now."

Lynn stared at Cole, then at the seat Marisa had just left. Lynn's usual seat.

"Cole, look at my face. I swear to you that I am trying very hard to remain calm here. I am trying not to flip out, even though I think in a situation like this, flipping out would be a very, very understandable thing to do. I want you to know something — I know it's not your fault that these . . . people are in our house. I know it's not your fault that they have invaded our lives. And if I hate the position it puts us in, I want you to know without a doubt that this *in no way* means that I hate you or anything about you. Do you understand me?"

Cole nodded.

"I know you help these people," Lynn continued. "I know you are doing good. But let me tell you, if I could make your gift go away, I would do it in a second. I would sell this house, use every penny I own to make this stop. I would take you to any end of the earth . . . if only it would help."

Lynn took the pizza cutter from the drawer. "Now clear off the table. It's time to eat."

Cole thought the subject was finished, but as his mom sat down to eat, she asked, "Is she really fifteen?"

"Yes."

Lynn shook her head sadly. "I don't understand this world. I really don't understand it at all."

Cole tried to sleep, but the house was far from quiet. The dead people were content to leave him alone until morning, but their voices carried through the night — "It's all my fault" and *Skazhi im, chto ya etogo ne delal!*" and "Warren!"

Closer, but still outside the door, Marisa began to sing a song in lullaby tones:

Though far I go
In winter lands and oceans blue
The fairest winds
Will take my song and tell you true . . .

These were the last words Cole heard before he fell asleep. They infused his dreams and were still with him when he woke.

EIGHT

When Cole saw the broken-necked man waiting for him the next morning outside school, his stomach lurched. But the man didn't say a word. He just stared Cole down, then headed off.

Cole wasn't sure when he would be back.

He suspected it would be soon.

As the news of the crash intensified — this morning the reporters said a clue had been found on the flight recorder, but the FAA hadn't released their findings yet — Jason's and Cole's popularity grew.

"Yeah, we were interrogated for hours," Jason was telling the crowd this morning. "They think we might have seen something important."

Cole pulled Jason aside.

"They didn't *interrogate* us," he told his (best?) friend. "They just asked us questions."

"What's the difference?" Jason asked. "Anyway, so what if we make the story a little more exciting?"

"It's not the truth," Cole argued.

"The truth is *boring*," Jason said with a sigh. Now that his crowd was gone, he looked tired.

Cole decided to let the subject drop. In Mr. Retlin's class, he and Jason drew comics and passed them to each other. It was like before the crash, when they could spend whole periods thinking of ways to crack each other up.

But at lunch, things fell apart again. Marisa was with Cole; it was understood that he would visit the hospital after school. Jason was at his usual spot in the cafeteria, surrounded by a new crowd — or maybe just members of the old crowd who wanted to hear the story again. There was a seat left open next to Jason — a seat for Cole.

"The plane went right over the museum — I swear, if it had fallen any sooner, I wouldn't be here talking to you now. It just crashed into the ground with this big boom, and then it fell apart on the ground. The fire was everywhere. . . ."

"Awesome!" one kid exclaimed.

Cole looked at Marisa's face, her reaction. She'd closed down. She was trying not to hear.

"Stop it!" Cole found himself saying. "It wasn't awesome. Don't say that."

"What's your problem, Cole?" Tom, the kid who'd said "awesome," now asked.

"Nothing. I just want you to stop talking about it like it was cool."

"It *was* cool," Jason surprised Cole by saying.

Cole knew he should leave Jason alone. He knew Jason liked being popular — even if he was lying. The worst possible thing would be to argue with him in public.

But he couldn't be quiet with Marisa standing there.

"It *wasn't* cool, Jason," Cole said quietly. "More than a hundred people died."

He'd backed Jason into a corner. So now Jason pushed back.

Jason said, "Will you lighten up? I was just saying what I saw. If you saw something else, wait your turn."

"You tell him, Jason!" Tom added.

Jason and Cole matched looks for a second. Cole hardly recognized his friend.

Or maybe he just saw someone he hadn't ever known that well.

He walked out of the cafeteria without eating lunch. Marisa followed.

"Slow down," she called. He stopped.

"I'm sorry about what he said," Cole told her.

"Don't be. He can't help it. It's what he wants to think he saw. He's scared, Cole. He hasn't slept in two nights."

"How do you know?"

"I've seen him, Cole. I know."

Later in the day, Cole tried to make up with Jason. Maybe Marisa was right. Maybe this was Jason's way of dealing with things.

But whenever he tried to talk to him, Jason would brush him off. Clearly, he'd struck a nerve.

Cole waited at Jason's locker after school, hoping they could talk things out. Why should he have to lose a friend over this?

After ten minutes, Jason still hadn't shown. Cole headed to his own locker, opened it, and began to shove his books inside.

Suddenly, a voice intoned, *"Skazhi im, chto ya etogo ne delal!"*

Cole froze. Then he looked up.

But it wasn't the broken-necked man.

It was Detective Brown, in his suit and hat. His expression was dead serious. He wasn't playing games now.

"Can you tell me what that means, Cole?"

Cole shook his head.

"Do you know Russian?"

"No," Cole whispered. He could see other students passing by, shooting glances at him.

"Then why was this phrase written on your hand yesterday? Can you tell me that?"

"I don't know."

Detective Brown slammed Cole's locker shut. Cole jumped. The whole hallway was looking at him now.

"I'm losing my temper, son. And you don't want that. You're holding back some very important information. I'm going to ask you one more time — do you know what *'Skazhi im, chto ya etogo ne delal'* means?"

"No."

"I'll tell you then. It's Russian for, 'Tell them I didn't do it.' Now why would you have that written on your hand?"

"I must've heard it somewhere."

"Yes, Cole. But where?"

The cop was staring Cole down. But there was no way could Cole tell the truth.

"I can't remember," he mumbled.

"Speak up, Cole."

"I said *I can't remember*."

Detective Brown sighed deeply. "Cole, I'll tell you something that you might find hard to believe.

Or, maybe not that hard — but I think you hold the key to finding out why that plane crashed. Watch the news tonight and you'll know what I mean. Now, do you have anything else to tell me?"

"I'm sorry, sir," Cole mumbled, his eyes downcast.

"There's no need to be sorry unless you have something to be sorry for."

When Cole didn't respond, Detective Brown tilted his hat a little forward and said, "I'll be in touch."

Cole didn't watch him go. Instead, he opened his locker again and resumed putting his books in. He tried to ignore the looks from the other kids. He tried to pretend that nothing had happened.

He tried to pretend they weren't looking over and seeing a freak.

When Marisa walked over, he wasn't exactly happy to see her. It wasn't her fault, really. He just wanted to be left alone.

It was times like this when he missed Malcolm the most. The time they'd spent together had been special; nobody besides Cole's mom had ever cared so much about him and his problems. Dr. Crowe had shown Cole that not all dead people were bad. Most of them were just confused and full of longing. Everyone — both living and dead — had his or her own mysteries. Like it or not, it was Cole's calling to solve the mysteries of the dead.

But this mystery — the plane crash — was bigger than Cole could handle. There were too many people involved, too many conclusions that had not been reached. People who died of long illnesses — people who *knew* they were going to die — rarely bothered Cole. But people who were unaware — the people who died in accidents, or of gunshots, or in other random acts of violence — these were the people who would never let him rest. They had been torn from their lives; now they wanted at least a little bit back. Cole was the person they thought would give it to them.

He would if he could.

If not, the dead people wouldn't be happy.

They'd be mad.

NINE

Marisa met him after school. She must have sensed Cole's dark mood, since she stayed silent on their ride to the hospital. It was her way of giving him space.

There were fewer reporters today than there were yesterday — the story was growing old, there were other tragedies to swarm to. Still, Cole opted for the back entrance.

A nurse was ministering to Emily when Cole walked into the room. She eyed him carefully.

"Are you a friend of Emily's?" she asked.

Cole nodded.

"It's Thomas," Emily's mother said. "He was here yesterday."

"And where are your parents?" the nurse wondered.

"My mom's outside," Cole lied. "She didn't want to come in. She hates hospitals."

"An honest woman," Emily's mother observed. "I like that. Most people try to think of a more elaborate excuse. My sister was just here, wasn't she?"

"Emily's aunt was just here," the nurse said. "All the way from California."

"She would have been here sooner," Emily's mom explained, "but they were away on vacation. I called and I called and I called — no response. Finally, word got through to her and she came here with her boyfriend, who seems nice enough."

"How's Emily doing?" Cole asked.

"It's hard to tell," the nurse answered. "She's better than she was yesterday, but she's not out of the woods yet. But she's strong —"

"Very strong," Emily's mother put in.

"— and young, which is good in a case like this."

"Can she hear what we're saying?"

"Different people have different opinions," the nurse replied, "but I think she does. I think she's listening to us right now. Talk to her. Maybe that can help her be strong."

The nurse left the room. Emily's mom began to

hum a tune — the same tune that Marisa had been singing the night before.

"What's that song?" Cole asked.

"Was I singing?" Emily's mom said absently. "I guess I was. It's a song I used to sing to Emily and Marisa when they were little. It was a song I learned at camp. It was Emily's . . . favorite."

Emily's mom was crying again now. Cole felt bad.

"The nurse said she's getting better," he offered.

"I know, I know. It's just so hard, sitting here. I was supposed to be on that plane, Thomas. I was supposed to be sitting with her. But I was so afraid of flying that I backed out. I was . . . actually looking forward to having a few days to myself. Can you believe it? And now . . . this."

Cole tried to put himself in Emily's mother's shoes, but all he could manage was to put himself in his own mother's shoes. What would she be like if this had happened to him? Cole knew — she'd be devastated. There were no words to make it better.

"Look at me," Emily's mom continued, laughing a little at her own crying. "You came here to see Emily, and now I'm burdening you with all of my problems. How about I leave the two of you alone for a moment? I haven't really eaten all day. Maybe I'll pop down to the cafeteria for something."

Cole didn't want to be alone with Emily. It felt

creepy — besides what could he really say to her? But he couldn't argue with her mom.

Once she was out of the room, Cole approached the bed. Emily's burns were healing slowly. Her hair was in patches on her head and the skin on her face looked almost plastic. At least you could tell she was a girl — despite the harsh disfigurement, her expression was at peace. She was as innocent as breath.

Cole began awkwardly, "My name's Cole, not Thomas. You don't actually know me. I know your sister, Marisa. And I guess I know your mom. They both love you a lot and they want you to get better. We all want you to get better. My mom and I, even though we don't really know you, we pray for you every night."

Cole stopped then. What else could he tell her? Should he tell her about the crash? Probably not, even if Emily was the one true living eyewitness. So he talked about other things. He talked about making pizza, and passing notes in school, and going to the movies with his newfound friends — all the things she might want to come back for.

The door opened and Emily's mom returned to the room.

"I got down to the cafeteria and realized I wasn't that hungry, after all. I have no appetite anymore.

Plus, my sister will be back soon, and she'll probably bring food. Did the two of you have a nice talk?"

Cole nodded. He wondered if Emily had heard a word he said. How strange, that dead people and living people could hear him — but he didn't know about the in-between.

Marisa was waiting for him in the hallway. Obviously, her mom hadn't been able to see her when she'd walked to the cafeteria. Cole knew enough not to raise the subject.

"I'm going to stay here tonight," Marisa told him. "I'll see you back here tomorrow, right?"

"Right."

Cole was worried — because he knew he was going to miss Marisa's company on the ride home.

I shouldn't be missing dead people. I should want them to go.

Before things could get more complicated, Cole took off. He noticed that the man who'd called out "Felicia" was no longer by the hospital. Maybe he'd found her, after all.

Or gave up.

Cole walked alone to the bus stop. Suddenly, the air was pierced by a haunting shriek. Instinctively, Cole turned in the direction of the noise. He saw a woman in a bloody uniform, screaming as loud as she could. Cole tried to turn away, but it was too late.

She'd seen him.

And she knew he'd seen her.

"You!" she called. She was coming toward him now, wobbling awkwardly because of her broken bones and broken shoe heels. One of her elbows protruded from her skin. She was wearing a flight attendant's outfit, ripped to shreds.

"You see me!" She was in Cole's face now. The other people at the bus stop didn't notice her. "I have been screaming here for two whole days, and you are the first person to hear me and see me. What are you? Where am I? WHAT AM I DOING HERE?"

There was a crazed look in her eyes. Cole tried to back away, but she was with him step for step. He hit the glass shelter of the bus stop. The other people started to watch him.

"Look at my nails," the flight attendant wailed, holding out her hands. Each of her fingernails was broken. "Look at this." She ran her jagged nails over her face, leaving trails of blood. Cole flinched. "I can't feel a thing," she continued. "Tell me — WHY CAN'T I FEEL ANYTHING?"

Cole shook his head. He wasn't going to tell her. He was afraid to tell her.

"I don't know," he whispered, hoping the other people in the bus shelter wouldn't hear him.

"What if I do it to you?" The flight attendant scratched her nails across Cole's arm, digging in. Cole screamed, feeling them cut through his shirt and into his flesh. His knees gave way and he fell to the ground.

"Are you okay?" one of the people in the shelter said.

"Is it a seizure?" another asked.

"TELL ME," the flight attendant screamed. "TELL ME THE TRUTH!" She lunged her fingers for his heart.

He had no choice. His heart was pounding wildly, his throat went dry.

"You're dead," he said. "You died in a crash."

The flight attendant stumbled back, retreated.

"NO!" she protested.

"You already knew it," Cole whispered. "I'm only telling you what you already knew."

"Who's he talking to?" the first person in the bus shelter said.

"Damned if I know," the other replied.

"Why am I still here?" the flight attendant asked now.

"I don't know," Cole whispered . . . and she realized this was the truth.

"It's her, isn't it?" the flight attendant replied.

"It's because I didn't stop her. It must be. It's all my fault."

"What's your fault?" Cole asked, squeezing his eyes shut.

"The crash. Everything. It's because I didn't stop her! THIS IS MY PUNISHMENT."

Cole wanted to ask her more. But she was running away now, still screaming.

It was only when she was gone and the bus had pulled up that Cole realized his arm was bleeding. The other passengers were now keeping their distance.

"What happened?" the driver asked.

Cole wished he could explain, but nobody would ever believe it.

So instead he ignored the driver and showed his pass.

Luckily, he got home about five minutes before his mom. He rushed to the bathroom and cleaned up his arm. Then he threw the torn shirt under his bed and took out a new one. He'd have to wait until just the right time to show his mom — after the dead people from the crash were gone.

Or I'll just throw out the shirt. It won't be the first time.

He heard the door opening just as he was slipping on the new shirt. He could also hear the cries for Warren and the burned man stumbling through the laundry room.

"Cole?" his mom shouted out.

"In here, Mom!"

"Are you okay?"

Cole shoved the old shirt deeper under the bed. "I'm fine!"

He heard his mom go into the living room and switch on the TV. The room was filled with the sound of news.

"You'd better come see this!"

Cole headed to the living room. Neither Gwen nor the wall-clinging man were paying attention to the TV. But when Cole saw it, his blood ran cold.

Right on the screen was the face of the broken-necked man.

Under it was one word: SUSPECT.

TEN

"To repeat our top news story," the anchorman spoke, "there have been a number of breakthroughs today in the crash of Flight 333. Here with a full report is Zach Simko."

"Thank you, Jim. I am here at the crash site, where the news has been nonstop since the press conference an hour ago. This is what we know: The cockpit recorder clearly indicates that someone *walked into the cockpit* right before the plane went down. The pilot is heard telling the intruder to get out, but there is no sign that he does. Then there is shouting . . . followed by the crash.

"Based on the information on the recorder, the authorities have named Yuri Chernenko as a suspect. Of course, Chernenko died in the crash with the others."

"Zach," the anchorman asked, "could you tell us why Chernenko is the suspect?"

"That is unclear right now, Jim. But our sources say it may have to do with the plane's history. It was revealed today that the plane that went down is the same plane that was attacked by terrorists four years ago. Officials at Golden Globe Airlines have refused to confirm this, but our sources are pretty solid."

The camera now cut to the anchorman, who addressed the viewer.

"As you recall, Flight 165 was hijacked four years ago by three terrorists, led by Alexi Voltarin, also known as The Fox. They demanded the release of four other jailed terrorists. A multinational force liberated the plane, resulting in the death of Voltarin and the other two terrorists, as well as one passenger."

The screen cut to four years ago, with video footage of the liberation of Flight 165 — the troops attacking, the sound of gunfire, the frightened faces of the escaping passengers.

The camera now was back on the reporter.

"Jim, it is a theory going around here now that Chernenko could have been a member of the terrorist organization, exacting a payback by crashing the same plane that the other terrorists died on. While we know that Chernenko and Voltarin were both of Soviet descent, the terrorist organization itself was never tied to a single country or government. The two other terrorists killed on Flight 165 were from other regions. Of course, Chernenko's involvement in this group is just a theory. But as the evidence continues to be sifted, the fingers are definitely pointing in Chernenko's direction — especially if the flight recorder has some indication that he was in the cockpit at the time of the crash."

The picture of Chernenko was shown again — a dead-eyed passport photo, which took on the menace of a killer.

Lynn switched off the TV and studied Cole's face.

"I need to know this, Cole," she said. "Has he been here?"

Cole nodded.

"In this house."

"Yes."

"That's it!" Lynn was out of her chair now, pacing furiously. "We can't stay here. I don't know what he's going to do to you."

Cole tried to stay calm, even though he was feeling the cold terror, too.

"He'll find us," he said quietly. "We might as well stay here."

There was a crash from the kitchen.

"What now?" Lynn screamed, rushing out of the room. Cole followed her.

All Lynn could see was the cereal bowl shattered on the floor.

Cole could see the burned man crawling over the shards, running his hand over the floor and up the leg of the kitchen table.

"Is it him?" Lynn asked.

"No, it's another one."

Cole's mom looked like she wanted to smash something, too. But she didn't. Instead she tried to make a joke.

"Listen to us, baby, we're just a regular, ordinary family, right? You, me, and a few ghosts. A regular *Brady Bunch*."

"It's okay, Mom," Cole reassured her. "I like our family."

Lynn shook her head. "Cole, sometimes I wish I could be as strong as you."

At that moment, Cole felt anything but strong. Did it count if you were being strong only because you were afraid of what would happen if you weren't?

There was a sudden silence in the house. At first,

Cole couldn't figure out why. Then he realized: Gwen had stopped calling for Warren. He left his mom in the kitchen to check it out. Gwen was still at the window, but she looked sadder now, even more forlorn.

"We'll find him," Cole whispered.

Gwen didn't acknowledge him. Nor did she show any signs of moving.

She would stay until Warren found her.

Cole would be sure not to tell his mom about *that*.

ELEVEN

Cole's room was freezing. It was impossible to fall asleep. The burned man was wandering from wall to wall, stepping on Cole's bed and knocking the papers off his desk. When he started to pull Cole's books off his bookshelf, Cole got up — he'd never get to sleep if he didn't confront the man first.

He had to be careful. Dead people didn't like to be interrupted. They usually preferred to be the ones to present their own problems — things could get ugly if they were forced to reveal their secrets directly.

Cole turned the lights on. *Try not to frighten him. Try not to be frightened.* The man didn't seem to notice. Cole blocked his path and he finally stopped circling.

"What do you want?" Cole asked. *What do I have to do to make you go away?*

The man looked at him curiously, unfocused. He didn't say a word.

"What's your name?" Cole tried again. "I'm Cole."

This approach didn't work, either.

"I can help you," Cole appealed.

The man pushed Cole aside with a bloody, scabbed palm.

He left no mark.

Cole sighed. There was no way to make dead people talk if they didn't want to. There was no question that the man *saw* Cole. But there was no way to know when — if ever — he would present his problem.

Cole gave up and crawled back into bed. He tried to remember Marisa's song:

Though far I go
In winter lands and oceans blue . . .

He couldn't remember the rest of the words. He wondered how it finished.

He wished Marisa was around to ask.

He started to sing other songs to himself, anything to drown out the footsteps and the sound of objects falling around his room. His teeth chattered from the cold — and the fear. He buried himself under all the blankets and eventually fell asleep.

He dreamed that he and Jason were standing again at the window, hearing the noise of the approaching airplane. But this time when he looked outside, he saw the plane was coming right toward them. Jason bolted and tried to pull Cole along. Cole wouldn't move. He had to watch. His own death was coming right at him. He was ready for it.

Suddenly, he was being lifted, choking for breath. All the air was gone. The air was turning black.

Cole woke up with a hand around his neck. He was being pushed against his bedroom wall, fingers cutting off his airway. He fought for his life.

"*Skazhi im, chto ya etogo ne delal!*" Chernenko yelled, his face twisted in rage.

"I can't!" Cole sputtered, desperately clinging to consciousness. *Make it stop*, he prayed. *Please make it stop.*

Chernenko's grip tightened.

"*Tolko ty mne mozhesh pomoch,*" he insisted.

"I CAN'T UNDERSTAND YOU!" Cole gasped. *Make it stop. MAKE IT STOP!*

Suddenly, Chernenko dropped Cole back into his bed.

"*Ya nevinoven. I ty dolzhen dokazat eto,*" he said.

"I. don't. speak. Russian," Cole tried to get across. "*Nyet! Nyet!*"

Cole felt something move under his bed. He looked down to find the burned man picking up the shirt that the flight attendant had torn. He began to try it on.

"*Nyet!*" Chernenko echoed. "*Ya ne prestupnik.*"

Cole wanted to keep him calm. He wanted to stop himself from shaking.

But he couldn't.

He remembered what Detective Brown had said — before, Chernenko had been saying "tell them I didn't do it."

Maybe if he thinks I'm on his side, he'll leave me alone.

It was his only chance.

"I will help you," he pleaded. "I will tell them you didn't do it. I will try to make them believe me."

"*Ya eshchyo vernus,*" Chernenko said, stalking out of the room.

The burned man began to overturn Cole's bed — even though Cole was still in it. Cole sprung out at just the right time.

This was it. The breaking point. *I can't take this anymore. I can't stay here.* Cole looked at the clock — two A.M.

I can't stand this alone.

He walked into his mom's room. He had sworn he'd never do it again, but now he needed to. There was nowhere else to go.

Lynn sensed him coming in. Whether she was asleep or awake, her mother sense kicked in.

"What is it?" she asked before Cole could say a word.

"Can I sleep in here tonight?"

"Of course you can."

Cole pulled off some blankets and slept on the floor. Lynn studied him in the moon-black darkness, trying desperately to find a way to help.

The clock ticked on.

Gwen began to pound on the window and cry.

Cole and his mom lay still.

Neither of them slept.

TWELVE

Jason wasn't surrounded by a crowd the next morning in school. He was waiting alone for Cole.

"I have to talk to you," he said.

Cole followed him into an empty classroom. He didn't know whether he was in trouble with his best friend or forgiven.

Jason closed the door behind them.

"Did you see the news this morning?" he asked.

Cole nodded. The authorities were still trying to find evidence that tied Chernenko to Voltarin and the other terrorists. The data on the flight recorder had yet to be released.

"Do you think that guy really did it?"

That guy. What would Jason think if Cole told

him *that guy* had been in his house last night, with his hands around Cole's throat?

"I don't know," Cole replied. "I guess."

Jason looked down at his sneakers for a second. Cole realized that he wanted to talk about more than the news.

"Cole," Jason said, "do you see them? Because I see them."

Cole's mouth went dry.

"See who?" he murmured.

"The people from the plane. They're in my nightmares every single night. It's like I'm on the plane with them and we're all going down. Or they're all burned and pulling at me, yelling why I didn't stop the crash." When Cole didn't respond, Jason continued. "You're the only person I can tell. Because you were there. My parents are about to freak out. They know I'm not sleeping, so I tell them I'm sneaking out of my room to watch the news. But that's not it. Do you know what I mean?"

Cole nodded.

"'Cause, tell me it's happening to you, too?" Jason asked hopefully.

"Sort of," Cole replied carefully.

"I knew it! It's what you said yesterday — I'm sorry about all that. I was talking about the crash that way because that's how everyone wants to hear it. They don't want to hear about the dead people. And I didn't want to *talk* about the dead people."

Cole wanted to look into his friend's eyes, but he couldn't. There were so many thoughts going through his head. There were so many things he could say to Jason. *I know what it's like to live nightmares. I know how scary it is. I know why you're scared. And you have no idea how scared I am. You have no idea what it's like to have nightmares when you are awake. You have no idea how lucky you are to be able to wake up and have the dead people go away.*

"You look really tired, too," Jason observed.

"I didn't sleep a whole lot, either." That much Cole could say.

"We look a little like ghosts ourselves," Jason joked. Then he became more serious. "Do you think the nightmares will stop?"

"Probably."

"I thought so."

They were quiet for a moment. The first bell rang.

"Don't tell anyone, okay?" Jason asked.

"I won't," Cole said.

It was nice to keep somebody else's secrets for a change.

The day was pretty normal — until Mr. Retlin's class.

They were still in their art history unit, and Mr. Retlin was talking about something called sur-realism. He turned off the lights to show some slides.

The first slide showed a desert landscape filled with melting clocks.

"This is perhaps the most famous surrealist painting," Mr. Retlin said, his voice a little awed. "It's called *The Persistence of Memory*. It's by an artist named Salvador Dalí."

Cole was intrigued by the painting. He knew how the melted watches would feel.

Mr. Retlin switched the slide, and in the flash of the switch, Cole saw the dead flight attendant in the doorway.

Even though the door was closed, she'd gotten into the room.

"There you are!" she shouted. "I saw the school insignia on your bag."

Cole tried to ignore her. A new slide appeared on the screen. A sky filled with bowler-hatted men, falling like raindrops. Falling — yet frozen in time.

"This is by René Magritte, another famous surre-alist. As you can see, surrealism is when ordinary objects take on extraordinary situations. Watches melt in a desert. Businessmen fall from the sky."

"I want to know why I'm still here. I WANT YOU TO TELL ME."

"Magritte was Belgian. Here's another painting of his, with a train coming out of a fireplace."

"If I'm dead, then why am I still here? Is it because of her? Is it because I let her in?"

"This painting is called *The Dominion of Light.* Note how the brushwork makes the objects almost seem real. And yet they are not real. Magritte himself showed this in the next painting I have for you . . ."

"TELL ME WHAT I HAVE TO DO!"

"Can anyone tell me what *'Ceci n'est pas une pipe'* means?"

She was on him now, hovering over his desk.

"Go away," he whispered urgently, trying to remain absolutely still.

"Not until you tell me how I *can* go away." The flight attendant struck out with her nails at Cole.

"It means 'This is not a pipe.'"

Cole moved away just in time, slamming his books off his desk. The whole class stared.

"Cole?" Mr. Retlin asked.

"Go away," Cole repeated, not hearing his teacher. "Leave me alone!"

"What did you say Cole?"

"I will NOT go away. Not until you tell me what I have to do!"

The flight attendant took a swipe at him again. Cole jumped out of his chair.

"Stop it!" he yelled, forgetting where he was. He moved in front of the slide projector, his shadow projected onto the screen, a surrealistic painting covering his body.

Mr. Retlin turned on the lights.

"What is going on?!?" he demanded angrily.

Jason jumped up onto his chair.

"Ohmigod!" he yelled. "It's a rat."

"A rat!" Eduardo chimed in.

Soon everyone was on their chairs, looking at the ground.

"I don't see a rat," Mr. Retlin said flatly. "Except, perhaps, standing on one of the desks."

The flight attendant backed away from Cole in all the chaos. He knew she'd return.

Once everyone was back in their seats, Mr. Retlin sent Cole and Jason to the principal's office.

It was the first time in his life that Cole had ever been accused of being a ringleader. He felt . . . kinda good.

"Do you care to tell me what exactly happened in Mr. Retlin's classroom?" the guidance counselor, Ms.

Keller, asked. They'd been sent to her by the principal's secretary.

"I thought I saw a rat," Cole said solemnly. "It was dark in the room, and I felt something run over my foot."

"Yeah, then it came over to me," Jason seconded.

Ms. Keller sighed. "There hasn't been a rat in this school in . . . at least five years."

"I saw one last year," Jason volunteered.

"Did you report it?"

"No."

"Well, then there's no way to know for sure."

Ms. Keller stared at them hard from across her large desk. Cole studied the pictures of her children on her desk, and couldn't help but feel a little sorry for them.

"Do you think this incident could be related to your trauma?" she asked bluntly.

"No, ma'am," Jason said gravely. "I don't believe I have a trauma."

Cole fought the urge to laugh. It wasn't fair of Jason to be *funny* at this moment.

Ms. Keller wasn't laughing.

"This is serious," she said. "You disrupted a class and are seeing rats that don't exist."

"It might have been a mouse," Jason said in a helpful tone.

"Or a gerbil," Cole added.

"I will check with the science rooms and see if all their animals are intact," Ms. Keller said with a formal efficiency. "In the meantime, I want the two of you to think about what's just happened. I will see you again in a week, and we can discuss it. If you see any connection between the plane crash and what you just did, I hope you will illuminate me. And if you see any more rats, try to calmly point them out to the teacher rather than causing a ruckus."

"We will," Jason promised.

"Absolutely," Cole put in.

"Good. You may return to class."

Cole and Jason didn't go directly back to Mr. Retlin's lesson. They hung around the hallways for a little bit, joking around. For the first time since the crash, Cole felt happy.

"Hey," Jason said, "it's Friday. You free after school? We could rent a movie or something. You could even stay over."

Cole wanted to say yes so badly. But he knew he had to be at the hospital after school. And he knew it wouldn't be a good idea to sleep over at anyone else's house until the dead people went away.

"I can't," he answered. "I have to go somewhere else. Maybe next weekend?"

Jason nodded. Cole couldn't tell him where he was going.

He was grateful to his best friend for not asking.

THIRTEEN

Marisa was waiting outside Emily's room. Because he had to tell *someone*, he told her about everything that had been happening.

She looked shocked. She'd had no idea how trapped Cole was by the mysteries and angers of the dead people.

"Tell me again what the flight attendant said," she asked.

"She said 'Is it because of her? Is it because I let her in?'" Cole related. He saw a spark of recognition in Marisa's eyes. "Why? Does it remind you of something."

"Yes," Marisa said offhandedly. "A little."

Then it hit her.

"Oh, my God — I'm remembering now."

"Remembering what? Tell me."

"Right before the crash. I remember Emily getting out of her seat."

"And . . ."

Marisa shook her head. "That's it."

"Maybe she was going to the bathroom?"

"No. She saw something. In the aisle. And she just unbuckled her seat belt and stood up . . ."

"What else?"

"I can't remember. It stops for me there. I knew I was going to die. But I don't see anything else."

"You can't remember her coming back?"

"No."

"So it's possible . . . the flight attendant was talking about her? About Emily?"

"It's possible. But where did she go?"

Now, when Cole needed the flight attendant the most, she was nowhere to be found.

Cole had a thought. "Maybe the flight attendant saw she was out of her seat and tried to get her to sit down right before the crash. Maybe she didn't get to her in time. So now she's feeling guilty that your sister wasn't in her seat, and was thrown around in the crash. Maybe she's like you, and still here until your sister gets better."

"Could that be it?" Marisa asked hopefully.

Cole had to admit he wasn't sure.

"Why don't you come in and see Emily with me?" he asked her.

"I'd rather see her alone. I can't explain it. I can't go in with you."

"That's okay. I'll be back soon, then."

Cole pushed the door open and went into the room. He was happy to find it empty except for Emily's mother. She was on her knees, leaning against the side of the bed. At first Cole thought she was looking into Emily's eyes. Then he realized her own eyes were closed.

Cole tried not to disturb her. He kept his distance and looked at Emily, who was as peaceful as ever. He wished there was a way to get through to her — there were so many questions he wanted to ask. What had she seen? Where had she been when the plane crashed?

It was possible she knew the truth about the crash. It was possible that Cole was the only one who could get through to her.

He hoped she would wake up. And part of him feared for her to wake up. Because when she did, all of her peace would be gone. She'd learn about the crash, and that her family wasn't the way it used to be. She would wake up to an entirely changed world. In her coma, she didn't know enough to be afraid. Cole felt afraid for her.

"Hello, Thomas," Emily's mother said quietly. "Do you want to come over here and join me?"

Cole couldn't refuse. He knelt down beside Emily's mother. But instead of praying, she talked to him.

"Emily's always been a fighter," she said. "You could never make her do what she didn't want to do. We'd buy her presents, and if she didn't like them, she'd just push them aside. I bought her this wonderful pink sweater — pink was her favorite color — and when I gave it to her, she informed me that purple was her *new* favorite color, and that she wouldn't be wearing pink anymore. And she didn't. She was so stubborn. Sometimes it drove me mad. But now I am so glad we let her be that way — because that's what's going to save her. I look into her eyes now, and I can see she's fighting to get out. She's not going to let this be the end."

They stayed by the bed for a while, neither praying nor speaking. They listened to Emily breathe.

Cole felt a little less cold. Then the temperature plunged.

Chernenko entered the room.

"Ty ne sdelal togo, o chyom ya tebya prosil!" he roared.

He was headed straight for Emily.

Emily's mother sensed Cole's disturbance.

"What is it?" she asked. When Cole didn't answer, she said, "I'm getting help."

She ran from the room.

Chernenko barreled forward.

"Don't hurt her!" Cole pleaded. "She can help you."

Unless, of course, she had seen him do what he was being accused of . . .

Either Chernenko didn't understand, or didn't want to. He reached out for one of the cables that connected Emily to the life support.

"Pochemo ty ne knochesh mne pomoch?" he demanded.

"No!" Cole cried and dove forward. With all his might he pushed Chernenko back from the controls.

It was the first time he'd ever fought a dead person.

Chernenko swatted him away, pushing into a tray full of instruments. They clattered loudly to the floor.

Two nurses rushed in, with Emily's mother at their heels.

"What is going on here?" they said. One rushed to Emily. The other called for the guards.

There was no way for Cole to explain what had happened. They didn't see Chernenko leaving the room. All they saw was an eleven-year-old kid, disrupted equipment, and the half-turned dial on Emily's life support.

Then they discovered that Cole wasn't really Thomas, and he was really in trouble.

The guards took him away. The police arrived. He was allowed to call his mother.

She wasn't at home. The receptionist at work said she'd try to find her.

Cole didn't want to leave a message that he was at police headquarters, but he had no choice, 'cause that's where they were taking him.

Marisa watched as he was taken from the room. There was no way for him to explain.

She had to know that he'd never hurt Emily.

Right?

Her eyes showed confusion, not condemnation.

Inside the room, her mother couldn't stop crying.

The police planned to put a guard on the room.

But Cole knew no guard could keep Chernenko away.

FOURTEEN

They left him alone in an interrogation room to think things over.

Cole wasn't surprised when Detective Brown stormed in.

"I want *so badly* to be through with you," Detective Brown blasted. "But I'll tell you one thing — I am NOT through with you. Not until you explain yourself good and true."

It was just the two of them. The door swung shut.

"I wanted to see Emily," Cole began. "I kept thinking about her. So I snuck in. I didn't do anything wrong. I just tripped and fell."

"That's what you say." Detective Brown wasn't buying it. "But it wasn't your first time there, right?

I saw you there on Wednesday, too. The nurse saw you there on Thursday. You said you were a friend of hers."

"I lied."

"He admits it! That's one lie down and a few million to go, I'd say."

Detective Brown tilted his hat up a little so Cole could see the whites of his eyes.

"I've been looking into your files, Cole. I have to say, I've found some interesting things."

Cole tried not to squirm in his seat. Which was exactly what Detective Brown wanted him to do.

"Where do I begin, Cole? Could it be with your school records? They're quite interesting. Outbursts in class for no reason. Talking to yourself. Keeping to yourself. 'Antisocial behavior' they call it now. Some of your teachers thought you'd go ballistic at any moment."

"That was before," Cole defended himself.

"Before *what*, Cole?"

"I mean, it was a while ago."

"A few months ago, the behavior stopped being reported. I'll grant you that." Detective Brown stared him down. "But it didn't go away. Did it, Cole?"

Cole stayed silent.

"I have psychiatrists' reports, too. ADD, ADHD,

depression, schizophrenia — any diagnosis that they can throw at a kid, they tried to throw at you. None of them stuck. You were too different for a general classification.

"And then there's the hospital report," Detective Brown continued. "The time your mom brought you in — you'd been locked in some kid's closet. In the middle of a birthday party, if I remember correctly. It must've been some party. They had to sedate you. And they found some cuts and bruises on your body, possibly self-inflicted. Strangely, it was after this hospital visit that your school reports started to get better. Cause and effect? I don't know."

"Where's my mom?" Cole asked defiantly.

"Oh, she'll be here soon, I'm sure. I want to talk with you first. I have a story to tell you, and I'm not sure she'd understand it. But I suspect that you will. Do you want to hear it?"

Cole didn't answer.

"Good," Detective Brown said, as if he'd heard a yes. "This is a story about *my* family. Don't worry — I won't bore you by talking about my parents. They were very sweet, very quiet, very ordinary people.

"And then there was my brother, Arthur. He wasn't boring at all. He was two years older than I was. I looked up to him so much. He was *cool* when he was young. Very popular in the neighborhood. You couldn't get him down.

"Then things started to change. He was about your age — maybe a little older. He started to have conversations with people who weren't there. Sound familiar?"

Cole stayed silent. He hoped the cop wouldn't see him tremble.

Detective Brown was watching him the whole time, even as he spoke. "Since I was his little brother, I'd ask him who he was talking to. And he was very honest about it. He'd say he was talking to Grandpa. And I'd say, 'Grandpa Joe?' because Grandpa Joe lived downstairs from us. He'd say, 'No, Grandpa Eddie.' I'd tell him that Grandpa Eddie was dead, and he'd go, 'I know.'

"Now, you can imagine this disturbed more than a few people. My very sweet, very quiet, very ordinary parents didn't know what to do. Arthur seemed okay with it, so they let it slide a little. Then things started to turn nasty. Arthur started to look afraid. He wasn't talking to our grandpa anymore. No, all sorts of other people were visiting him. He didn't tell anyone, but I could tell.

"He started to withdraw. He lost all his friends. He was awake all night. He would scream at the wind. My parents stopped being so sweet, quiet, and ordinary. They took him to doctors they couldn't afford, and paid good money for advice that didn't work. Arthur started to get real low. He was thirteen by then."

Detective Brown paused and wiped his forehead. "Now, Arthur's problem was never diagnosed. Maybe we would have found the right doctor, someone who could've taken care of him. But before that could happen, Arthur skipped off. I can tell you the day — February first. I woke up and looked at the bed next to mine, and Arthur was gone. I knew immediately. I saw that his favorite shirt was gone from the drawer. His jacket was missing. His wallet was gone — and the money from my wallet was gone, too.

"I like to think that he believed he was sparing us, taking his problem away with him. He wasn't going to burden us any longer. Have you ever felt that way?"

Cole tried hard not to nod.

"I *know* you've felt that way," Detective Brown continued. "And you know what? It's wrong. The pain he would've caused by staying was nothing compared to the pain he caused by leaving. My mother, my father — none of us was the same again. We looked for him everywhere. Every holiday, every birthday, we'd hope for a call. My parents moved into a smaller apartment to pay for a detective. But we never saw Arthur again. I don't even know if he's alive. This was over thirty years ago."

There was a pause — Detective Brown wanted Cole to say something. But he didn't say a word. He felt like the air had been knocked out of him. He couldn't possibly be hearing what he was hearing.

How many times had he thought of running away? How many times had he cursed himself, as if it was all his fault?

How many times had he wanted it over, the visions gone?

"Now here's where I make the leap," Detective Brown continued. "Because I can't think of any other explanation. I hear you talking to people who aren't there. You've written a Russian phrase on your hand when you don't even know Russian — and it just so happens that our main suspect is a Russian terrorist. You visit Emily Mason in the hospital for no discernible reason — and yet when you're leaving the room, one of the guards *swears* he sees you making eye contact . . . with the wall.

"Now don't get me wrong — I understand why you wouldn't tell me about it. I understand why you keep it secret. But right now — like I said before — I think you hold the key to this crash. I know you're only a kid, but it could be in your power to solve this thing. You could put both the dead *and* the living at peace. So I'm coming at you straight up now. I know it isn't fair, but none of this is fair. Tell me — what do you see?"

There was so much to say that Cole couldn't say any of it. Before he could start to unravel how he felt, the door flew open and his mother came storming in.

"There you are!" she said, running over to Cole and ignoring Detective Brown.

It was only after she saw Cole was okay that she turned on the cop full-force.

"Tell me what's going on here?" she shouted. "What are you saying to my son?"

For the first time since he'd met Cole, Detective Brown was speechless.

FIFTEEN

Another policeman poked his head in the doorway.

"Everything okay?" he asked.

"No worries," Detective Brown answered. "I can handle it."

After the door closed, Lynn launched into the cop again. "What right do you have to drag my son here and question him without a lawyer or a parent?"

"Ma'am, he's not being charged with anything."

"Don't *ma'am* me, *sir*. If he's not being charged, then why did I have to leave my job early to pick him up at police headquarters?"

"Because he was found at Regents Hospital, in Emily Mason's room."

"That's the girl —"

"— in the coma. Yes."

Lynn backed off a little and looked questioningly at Cole. He'd have to explain later. All of it.

"Look," Detective Brown said soothingly, "I'm really here to help Cole. And I hope Cole can help me. I know about Cole's problems —"

"You have *no idea* about Cole's problems," Lynn shot back.

"Mom," Cole interrupted, "he does."

Lynn stopped short now. She couldn't believe what she was hearing.

"He knows about the dead people," Cole whispered.

"Oh, so you see them, too?" Lynn asked Detective Brown sarcastically.

"No, but my brother did."

Cole's mom had to sit down now. She'd lost all will to fight.

"So I'm right, Cole?" the detective asked.

Cole nodded.

Now it was Detective Brown's turn to sit down. He was trying to hide his surprise. "I thought so," he said, "but I wasn't entirely sure —"

"So what are you going to do about it?" Lynn interrupted.

"What do you mean, Ms. Sear?"

"I mean, who are you going to tell? You realize how serious this is, don't you? You realize that you hold this boy's future in your hands."

"I realize that," Detective Brown said solemnly. "And I don't plan to violate his trust."

Lynn looked unsure, but there wasn't much she could do at this point.

She'd have to trust the cop.

"Now let's start from the beginning," he said.

So Cole told him. He told him about Marisa's visit, and how she'd appeared at the museum. He told him about Gwen and Warren, and the two burned men in his house. He told him about the flight attendant's attacks. Most of all, he told him about Chernenko, the broken-necked man. He tried to remember every word the terrorist had said. Detective Brown wrote them all down.

As Cole spoke, he studied the detective's expression. He could tell that the man wasn't prepared to be so right about Cole. Every now and then his attention seemed to drift. Cole wondered if Detective Brown was thinking about his brother. He wondered if Detective Brown really understood what Cole and Arthur went through.

"Do you believe me?" Cole asked.

Detective Brown nodded. "I do, Cole. It just brings up a whole lot of other things, most of which don't have anything to do with you."

"They have to do with your brother?"

The detective nodded again, but said no more.

"So what do you think about what Cole's told you?" Lynn asked. "Is it what you were looking for?"

"I'm not sure," Detective Brown confessed. "Russian isn't my first-choice language, but from what I can make out, it sounds like Chernenko is trying to force Cole to prove he's innocent. Which doesn't mean he *is* innocent — in fact, Chernenko is probably trying to use Cole to create *the illusion* of his innocence, so he can die with everyone *thinking* he's innocent."

He turned to Cole. "Chernenko hasn't mentioned Voltarin or Frane or Mahkner, has he? Those are the other terrorists."

"No," Cole answered. "I don't think so."

"That's too bad. From what I hear, the Feds are having a devil of a time trying to link him up to the other terrorists. And if they can't do that, it's going to be hard to figure out a motive. Now, have any of the other ghosts said anything else to you about the crash?"

Cole shook his head. "Marisa doesn't remember it much — only that Emily was out of her seat.

Gwen won't talk about it, the guy with the ear says, 'It's all my fault,' and the burned guy doesn't say anything at all."

"Do you think the guy with the ear is confessing to the crash? Do you believe he thinks the crash was his fault?"

"I don't know."

"It could be a situation like the flight attendant's, where she thinks she's responsible, but is only indirectly responsible. I wish there was some way to know."

Detective Brown's eyes grew wider.

"What is it?" Lynn asked.

"I just thought of a way Cole could help us — he might be the only one who can. He can talk to the other eyewitnesses," Detective Brown said.

"You mean from the museum?"

"No . . . the ones on the plane."

"And where would you find *them*?" Lynn asked.

"I have an idea. With your permission."

SIXTEEN

Lynn Sear wasn't crazy about the idea of having her son tour a crash site looking for dead people, but when Cole implored her with his earnest eyes, she couldn't see any way to say no.

"Are you sure it will be safe?" she asked Detective Brown for the hundredth time.

"Absolutely. All of the human remains have been cleared out, along with most of the wreckage. There's not much left to see. But it's possible some of the victims are still there, waiting for something."

Lynn knelt down and studied Cole's face.

"Are you sure you want to do this, baby?" she asked.

"I'm sure, Mom. I have to."

Lynn stood back up. "Okay, then. Just make sure he's home in time for dinner."

Detective Brown was certain it would be easier to smuggle Cole into the secure crash area than it would to bring both Cole and Lynn. It was going to be hard enough to get Cole in without anyone asking questions . . . questions that Detective Brown did *not* want to answer.

Cole got to ride in the front of the police car with Detective Brown. It was an unmarked car, anonymous blue, but the inside had a police radio and about a thousand empty coffee cups.

"Sorry about the mess," Detective Brown said as he cleared away a few days' worth of newspaper and fast-food wrappers. "My housekeeping's about as good as my Russian." He didn't say another word for a few more minutes.

"It's hard for your mom, isn't it?" he asked Cole.

Cole was looking out the window, at the city spreading around him. The sun was setting now — an early-winter sunset, painting the skyscrapers pink and amber.

"Yeah, it's hard for my mom," he told the detective.

"I've got to tell you something, Cole. I'll let you in on a secret that you probably know already. I've only known your mom for, what, a half hour? But I can see that whatever you throw her way, she can take it. She loves you that much."

"I know," Cole whispered. It's just that sometimes he forgot.

"My mom couldn't really take it. I think Arthur knew that."

Cole wanted to ask more about Detective Brown's brother — what he'd been like, how he'd handled his "gift." But he could sense that the cop would only go there when he wanted to.

The whole park area in front of the museum, as well as most of the sidewalks surrounding it, had been cordoned off by the police and the FAA. Detective Brown parked on the side of the road and flashed his badge to get them both inside. But they still weren't safe yet.

"What are you doing here?" a voice asked. Agent Masino was coming at them. He didn't look happy. Agent McCrum followed in his wake.

"What's the meaning of this?" Agent Masino was asking Detective Brown now.

"I'm just trying to jog the boy's memory," the cop answered. "He says he might remember more of what he saw. We were just going to walk up to the steps of the museum. Check out the view from there."

As Detective Brown finished his sentence, there was a surge of noise, and suddenly the area was lit by hundreds of spotlights. The night shift had begun.

"How many times have I told you, Detective, this is *not* your investigation." Agent Masino fumed. "It is *our* jurisdiction. We're more than happy to work with you people, but not like this. Bringing a boy here! Do his parents know?"

"His mother gave permission."

"Well, that doesn't reflect well on her, does it? There's no reason for him to be here. Get him out of my sight. I don't want to turn around and see him here again."

With that, Agent Masino stormed off. Agent McCrum remained where she was.

"What are you up to, James?" she asked.

"Just what I said, Ellen," Detective Brown replied, this time with a glimmer of a smile.

Agent McCrum shook her head. "I don't believe you . . . but I *do* trust you. I can keep Masino busy, but only for a little bit. Do what you have to do — and *don't* touch anything. You have ten minutes, tops. And you'll have your tape tomorrow."

"You are too good to me."

"I'm just hoping that one day it'll pay off."

Detective Brown gestured Cole forward.

"Take a good look around. Extra points if you find someone who was in the cockpit. If the flight recorder holds the information that the Feds say it does, then the cockpit was where something went wrong. Find the pilot or the copilot, and he might solve our mystery."

There were still dozens of people scouring over every inch of the site, trying to find even the most minute piece of wreckage, hoping it would provide a clue to the crash. Cole watched these figures working steadily, each one casting a stark shadow because of the spotlights.

Cole was looking for the ones who didn't cast a shadow.

The biggest pieces of wreckage had already been removed, shipped to a nearby empty warehouse, where the investigators would painstakingly try to piece it all back together again.

Remnants from luggage were scattered across the ground. Cole saw a key on the ground, its tip melted to a drop. He saw a fleck of blue jeans. A bottle cap.

Things that had once belonged to people on the plane.

Things that would never be reclaimed.

"Don't think about it, Cole," Detective Brown said, his voice concerned. "Put it aside right now.

The only thing you can do for them now is find out the truth."

Near the center of the wreckage, Cole spied an old man sitting in the fetal position, rocking back and forth as investigators walked right past him.

"I see one," Cole whispered.

Detective Brown stopped. "Where?"

Cole pointed. "There."

"Can you talk to him?"

Cole gulped back his fear. "I can try."

He felt like he was interfering.

But he didn't have a choice.

The investigators moved on to another part of the site. Cole stepped forward. Detective Brown was at his side, mystified.

"Hello?" Cole whispered as he got close to the man.

No response.

"Sir?" Cole tried again.

This time the man stopped rocking. He looked Cole right in the eye.

"I was sitting right here," he said.

Cole wondered what part of the plane had been here. He studied the man's clothes, trying to avoid the gaping wounds. He didn't seem to be wearing a uniform. It was unlikely the man had been in the cockpit.

But Cole couldn't just walk away because the man wasn't who he was looking for. He couldn't just abandon him.

"Where on the plane were you sitting?"

The old man laughed harshly. "*On* the plane? Ha! I was sitting *under* the plane. Just sitting in the park, minding my own business, I was. No way to get out of the way when a plane comes down, I tell you."

Cole nodded.

The man's expression grew serious.

"I need you to help me," he said.

"How?" Cole asked. As he did, he saw more figures coming forward.

Dead people.

"There are a lot of them," he murmured to Detective Brown.

"What is the man saying?"

"He wasn't on the plane."

The old man had gone back into his rocking motion. He'd forgotten Cole was there. His thoughts had taken him captive once more.

The same wasn't true for the other dead people.

There were three of them now. All speaking at once.

"Where's my Mary?" a thin man asked, the flesh peeling from his bald head.

"It's in the vault, Henry! It's in the vault!" a heavy woman with red hair yelled, her hipbone visible.

"W-w-where am I? Who can t-t-tell me w-w-where I am?" another woman, younger, asked.

All three looked like passengers. Cole couldn't tell if they knew they were dead.

"Were any of you in the cockpit?" he asked gently.

"I only travel business class!" the bald man shouted.

"Th-th-the c-c-cockpit?" the younger woman asked, not comprehending.

"He has to look in the vault!" the heavy redhead belted out.

"We don't have much time," Detective Brown cautioned.

"I don't think they can help," Cole said. All the dead people were looking at him now. Studying him.

Remembering him.

Cole could feel himself sweating, even though the night air was starting to chill.

They'll find me, he thought. *They'll all find me, wherever I go.*

"Do you know Warren?" he asked. But they were already beginning to wander off.

Detective Brown looked off in the distance. Cole followed his gaze.

Agent McCrum was sending them a signal, waving them away.

It was time to go.

Detective Brown quickly pulled Cole forward. They covered as much of the crash site as they could. Cole looked for people in airline uniforms — anyone who might have been in the cockpit.

He saw other dead people. But not the ones he was looking for.

Everyone — dead and living — looked up as he passed.

They knew he didn't belong.

He wondered if he'd ever belong — anywhere.

Detective Brown tried to console him on the car ride home.

"Well, it was worth a shot," the cop said. "We had to try. You're a very brave kid, Cole. You're helping me very much."

Cole wasn't really listening. He was thinking of the dead people . . .

So many dead people.

Every day, more and more. One at a time, or a hundred at once.

He would never escape them.

They would always recognize him, just as he would always be able to see them.

The rest of his life.

So many dead people.

"What's going on?" Detective Brown asked, aware that Cole had slipped away into thought.

"How can I do it?" Cole wondered aloud. "It's too much."

Detective Brown put his hand on Cole's shoulder. "I know it. Arthur knew it, too. But you know what I remember? For all the times that the dead people haunted him, there were other times when they left him alone. Those times seemed extra good. I can't say for sure, but I think they know when to hold back."

"Not now, they don't," Cole had to say.

"Then maybe I'm wrong. I hope I'm not."

Cole hoped so, too. He was looking forward to that extra good time, when he could be in control of his life again.

Right now, he'd be happy enough to survive.

SEVENTEEN

Cole's mom was waiting for them at the door.

"Five more minutes and he would've been late for dinner," she said to Detective Brown.

"I don't suppose you set the table for three?" Detective Brown replied with a grin, trying to pour on the charm.

"The only extra people in this house are dead people," Lynn shot back. "I don't suppose you'd like to join them?"

"*Mom.*" Cole was embarrassed.

"Sorry, honey. Would you like to stay for dinner, Detective Brown?"

"I'm afraid I can't. Have to stay on my case."

"As opposed to getting on our cases?"

Detective Brown grinned again. "Exactly." He

turned to Cole. "Now listen to me — I want you to be careful. Just because you didn't see Chernenko tonight doesn't mean he didn't see you. This could be a good thing, or it could be a bad thing. If it's a good thing, he'll think that you're trying to convince us that he's innocent."

"And if it's a bad thing?" Cole asked, scared now.

"Well, then he thinks the truth — that you're not out to help him at all. Let's just hope for the good news — and be on your guard tonight. Sleep in your mom's room. Scream if anything goes wrong. Call my cell phone at any hour if anything happens. I'll probably be at the station."

Detective Brown tipped his hat to both Cole and Lynn, then turned to leave.

"Detective Brown!" Lynn called after to him.

"Yes?" he said.

"Thanks. For believing him."

"Thank you for the same." He tipped his hat again, and was gone.

Cole and his mom went into the kitchen for dinner, passing by Gwen at the window. It was hard to eat with so much going on.

"Did you find what you were looking for?" Lynn finally asked.

Cole shook his head.

"Was it horrible? Are you okay?"

"I'm fine," Cole said.

"Tell the truth," a voice counseled him. It wasn't his mom; it was Marisa. She walked behind Lynn's chair, so Cole could look at them both at the same time.

"I'm worried about you," Lynn and Marisa said at the same time.

"This is too much," Lynn continued.

"You shouldn't be asked to do all this," Marisa said.

"I can handle it," Cole countered, but even his voice didn't seem to think it was true.

"I should leave you alone," Marisa murmured. "I should go."

"No!" Cole cried out. He knew Marisa wasn't talking about leaving the room for a moment — she was talking about leaving him forever.

"What is it?" Lynn asked, startled.

"It's Marisa. She wants to leave. I have to go talk to her."

Marisa had walked off toward Cole's room. He followed. She was looking at the books and CDs on his shelves.

"I had a room like this," she said. "A little bigger. Some of the same books, even. Loads of magazines — I loved magazines. We have different taste in music, but that's okay. You're younger than me, so your taste will get better."

She turned to Cole now, her glance taking him all in. Again, she seemed much older than her actual age. "I was a lot like you. With one big difference — if our roles were switched right now, I wouldn't even know you were there. I would walk right by you. I wouldn't see you at all."

Marisa thought for a second before continuing. "I don't think I could handle seeing the things you see. And I'm realizing it's unfair to ask you to help me. It's selfish. With so many other people coming after you, the last thing you need to worry about is me. I don't know why I thought you could help my sister. Maybe it's because you're the only person who could hear me, and I wanted to think that *I* could help her — through you. I don't know. But it should stop. I should say good-bye."

"Please don't," Cole said. "I like helping you."

"But I should be helping you back."

"You *are* helping me," Cole insisted.

"You're just saying that."

Cole looked her right in the eye. "I'm not. I like talking to you."

Something in Cole's expression made Marisa step back. She seemed to recognize something there. A connection.

"I have to go back to my sister," she said.

"But I'll see you tomorrow?"

Marisa nodded. "Yes."

"Promise."

"I promise."

Cole couldn't let her leave for good. Not yet. He needed her because she made him feel better about his sense. He needed her because the rest of the world was growing so crazy, and only she seemed to understand.

Once she was gone, he returned to the kitchen. He and his mother finished dinner, then watched the latest reports on TV. The news channels were full of stories about Chernenko — reporters had trekked to his hometown in Russia and were cross-examining people who hadn't really known him well. The only thing they knew about him was his violent temper and his tendency to keep to himself. Nobody could remember an association with Voltarin or the other terrorists. But they said they wouldn't be surprised if he'd led a secret life.

"I'm going to go in my room and watch my shows," Lynn announced. "Come in when you're ready for bed. I've already set up your sleeping bag and your tent."

"Thanks, Mom."

Cole slunk back on the couch and flipped more channels, hoping one of them would teach him something he didn't already know about the crash. He glanced over to Gwen, who was crying again. The burned man stumbled past her, running his hand over the window, then falling to the floor with barely a groan.

After a few minutes, Cole turned off the TV. He went over to Gwen.

"I looked for him," Cole said soothingly. "I'll keep looking for him."

"Warren!" Gwen sobbed.

"Yes, Warren. I'm going to find him for you, Gwen."

Cole noticed a shift in the room. The burned man on the ground had fallen still.

He was looking at Cole now with glassy eyes.

"Did you say Warren?" he asked.

"Yes," Cole answered.

"And Gwen?"

"Yes." Cole's throat was going dry.

"Well, I'm Warren," the man said. "Where's Gwen?"

"She's . . . right here."

"I don't see her."

"I promise you, she's right here."

Warren looked very confused.

Cole turned to Gwen, who couldn't hear a word Warren said. He had to think of something.

"Gwen," Cole said. "I need you to tell me something that only Warren knows. I think I've found him."

"Warren?!?" Gwen screamed. "Where's Warren?"

"Listen to me, Gwen. I need you tell me something that only Warren knows."

"I don't know . . . our first date was to see *Grease*."

Cole turned to Warren.

"Warren, Gwen is right here. She's telling me your first date was to see *Grease*."

"Gwen! I can't see her. I've lost my glasses. I can't see a thing."

"That's okay, Warren. Now I need to know something from you that only Gwen would know."

"My nickname for her is Lady. From *Lady and the Tramp*."

"Gwen, does Warren call you Lady? Like from *Lady and the Tramp*?"

Gwen was sobbing now, barely making out a "yes."

"Tell her I love her," Warren asked.

"Gwen," Cole said. "Warren wants you to know that he loves you."

"Tell her I'll always love her."

"He'll *always* love you."

120

"Tell him . . . tell him I love him, too."

"Warren, she wants me to tell you that she loves you, too."

"Always."

"*Always.*"

"Why can't she tell me herself?" Warren asked. Then Cole saw it — the realization spread across Warren's face.

Suddenly, he knew.

Reality hit.

"Oh, my God!" he gasped.

Cole turned to Gwen.

He looked at her expression and saw that she had already known.

She'd just been waiting.

Waiting for Warren.

"It's okay," she said. "Tell him it's okay."

Cole walked over to Warren.

"She wants you to know it's okay. It's all going to be okay."

Gwen was looking over at him now. She was following Cole's glance to where Warren was.

"Can you leave us alone for a second?" she asked.

Cole nodded and left the room.

When he returned ten minutes later, they were both gone.

EIGHTEEN

Detective Brown called at eight the next morning.

"Sorry to wake you," he said.

Since it was Saturday, Lynn was still asleep.

"I need you to come down here right now," the detective told Cole. "I think we might be onto something."

"Okay," Cole mumbled.

Then he woke his mom up and asked for a ride to the police station.

Once Lynn had reluctantly left, Detective Brown asked him how the night had been.

"Any visits from our friend Chernenko?" he asked.

"No," Cole was happy to be able to reply.

"Good," Detective Brown continued as a technician wheeled in a set of speakers. "Our friend Agent McCrum was kind enough to supply the department with a copy of the tape from the cockpit recorder on Flight 333. As you know, the tape hasn't been released yet to the media. I want to play it for you and hear what you think. Pay close attention."

The technician pressed a few dials and the speakers were filled with sound.

"... *bearing Southeast. ... Oh, hello. I'm afraid you can't come in here. Why don't you go back to your seat ... wait — what are you doing? What's going on?!?*"

Then static.

"Now, the person who walks into the cockpit doesn't say anything," Detective Brown notes. "Could you hear anything?"

Cole shook his head.

"Me, neither. But that's why the FAA doesn't count on our ears. When they amplified it, they heard something else."

The technician hit a button.

Cole listened to the cockpit voices again.

"... *Oh, hello. I'm afraid you can't come in here. Why don't you go back to your seat ... wait — what are —*"

"Stop!" Detective Brown interrupted. "Did you hear anything?"

"I don't think so."

"Listen between 'seat' and 'wait.'"

The technician replayed the tape.

This time Cole heard it — a slight murmur. A low-voiced garble.

"You hear it, don't you?" Detective Brown asked.

"Yes."

"What does it sound like?"

"Nothing really."

"Nothing in English, really. But the FAA is convinced it's Russian. *'Vy vse dorogo zaplatite za eto'* — translated as, 'You're all going to pay.'"

The technician played it again. This time, Cole could almost hear the words that Detective Brown had just said.

Almost.

But not so much that he'd be sure.

"I can tell you're wavering," Detective Brown observed.

"I'm not positive," Cole said. But it wasn't just that. It was something else. . . .

"Could you play it again?" he asked. "From the beginning."

The technician looked to Detective Brown for

approval. The cop, curious, nodded. His eyes didn't leave Cole.

The room filled once more with the dead pilot's voice.

"*. . . Oh, hello. I'm afraid you can't come in here. Why don't you go back to your seat . . . wait — what are you doing? What's going on?!?*"

"What is it, Cole?" Detective Brown asked. "Do you hear something else?"

Cole wasn't sure. "It's nothing," he said.

"No," Detective Brown insisted, "tell me."

"Well, it's the words."

"What do you mean?"

"It's what the pilot says at the beginning. It doesn't sound right."

"How so?"

"I don't know . . . It doesn't sound like he's talking to a big adult terrorist. If someone . . . threatening walked into a cockpit when I was flying, I don't think I would say 'Oh, hello' and 'I'm afraid you can't come in here.' It's almost like he's talking to —"

"— a kid," Detective Brown finished the thought. Cole nodded.

"And do you think it's —" Detective Brown asked.

"Emily."

"Chernenko could have come in afterward," Detective Brown said, pressing his hands onto the table. "Emily might have been in the cockpit when Chernenko came in. The pilot could have been talking to two separate people!"

"She's in danger," Cole whispered.

Detective Brown nodded.

They had to get to the hospital . . . before Chernenko returned.

EIGHTEEN

"Be careful," Cole's mom said to him as he and Detective Brown left the station. He could tell she didn't want him to go . . . but she knew that he had to.

Detective Brown put the siren on his car roof and sped to the hospital. In ordinary circumstances, Cole would have been thrilled to be in a cop car traveling at full speed; not even Jason would believe it.

Now Cole concentrated on learning what Detective Brown was trying to teach him — a few Russian phrases, just in case Chernenko showed up.

Cole didn't have to take the back way into the hospital this time. Luckily, most of the reporters were gone, so Detective Brown's arrival didn't get much attention. After waiting for the elevator for one minute too long, Cole and Detective Brown sprinted up the stairs. There was a police guard posted outside Emily's door — but no guard could keep a dead person away.

Detective Brown flashed his badge and greeted one of the guards by name. They didn't question Cole's presence. They just let him through.

Marisa was sitting on one side of Emily's bed; her mother was on the other.

"Hi, Cole," Marisa said, looking up. "There's good news."

"What are you doing here?" Emily's mother asked angrily. "You're not Thomas! You're an impostor. You almost hurt her yesterday!"

"I know I'm not Thomas," Cole said. "But I'm here to help."

"I'm going to call the police."

"There's no need to do that. I promise you, I'm here to help Emily."

"Cole," Marisa asked, "who are you talking to?"

Cole looked her in the eye. How could he tell her?

How could he not?

"I'm talking to your mother," he said quietly.

"My mother?"

Cole nodded.

"She's here?!?" Marisa looked around frantically,

128

but the only people she saw were Emily, Cole, and Detective Brown, who was hanging in the background. The ones who were alive.

Dead people can't see other dead people. They don't even know that they're there.

"She's been here all along," Cole said gently. He looked over at Marisa's mom and saw she thought he was talking to Emily.

Marisa was breathing deeply now, trying to keep calm.

"Does my mom know that she's dead?" she asked.

"No, she doesn't."

"Please don't tell her. It's better not to know."

"I know," Cole whispered. "I won't tell her."

"She's right here?"

"Right across the bed from you."

Marisa reached over the bed, over Emily's sleeping body, and touched her mother's face. It was a touch that neither could feel. But both of them knew. Marisa pulled her hand back, satisfied. Her mother looked right at her — not seeing her, but sensing her presence.

"The doctors say Emily's condition is improving," her mother said softly. "She could wake up at any moment now."

Then she began to sing:

Though far I go
In winter lands and oceans blue
The fairest winds
Will take my song and tell you true . . .

"Any sign of Chernenko?" Detective Brown asked.

Cole shook his head.

"What's she doing?" Marisa wanted to know.

"She's singing the song you sang."

"The camp song?"

"Yes."

Marisa began to sing the song, too, in a higher voice than her mother's, and one verse behind.

Cole looked into Emily's eyes.

Could she hear?

Was she listening?

He turned to Detective Brown.

"We need to sing to her," he said.

"Sing!" Detective Brown protested. "I may be James Brown, but I can't carry a tune in a bag. You're not going to get *me* to sing."

"It's for Emily."

"You're joking."

"No. Her mother and her sister are here, and they're singing. I don't know if Emily can hear them. We might be able to help."

"By singing?"

Cole nodded and told him the words.

And so they began. Four voices — all trying to bring Emily back to life.

Though far I go
In winter lands and oceans blue
The fairest winds
Will take my song and tell you true
You'll ever be in my heart
For I'll remember you . . .

They all watched Emily as they sang. They studied her every breath, waited for a slight flutter of her eyelids. Marisa held her left hand; her mother held her right. Cole leaned over and ran his fingers across her ragged hair.

"Wake up," he whispered. "We're all waiting for you here."

Then out of the corner of his eye, he saw another person enter the room. A person Detective Brown made no move to stop.

Because he didn't see him.

Chernenko.

Cole pulled back from Emily's bed, trying not to alarm her sister or her mother.

"He's here," he whispered to Detective Brown.

"Remember what I told you," the cop replied.

131

Chernenko was moving forward. Moving for Emily.

"Ona pomozhet tebe!" Cole cried.

She can help you.

Chernenko stopped.

"Ya znayu," he said.

"What does *'ya znayu'* mean?" Cole desperately asked Detective Brown.

"It means, 'I know.'"

"Cole, look!" Marisa called.

It was Emily.

She was waking up.

Chernenko stepped back. Cole went over to the bed.

Emily's eyes were opening.

She was looking around the room.

She was seeing everything.

She took a breath.

And then she said, "Mom!"

NINETEEN

"I'm right here," her mom answered.

Emily was looking right at her.

"What's going on, Cole?" Detective Brown asked.

Cole couldn't believe it.

"She *sees* them," he murmured.

Her head turned to Marisa.

"Marisa," she said, before losing her speech in a fit of coughs.

"You mean to tell me that she can see —" Detective Brown began.

Cole nodded.

Marisa looked confused.

"Is she dead?" she asked.

"No," Cole answered, trying to overcome his shock. "She's like me."

Emily's mother was crying with joy, embracing her tightly and telling her everything was going to be all right.

"Cole," Marisa said, "I'm scared."

Emily's mother was talking about going home, making pancakes, redecorating Emily's room.

She had no idea.

"It's over, isn't it?" Marisa continued. "I'm going to have to go now."

Cole didn't know what to say. He didn't want Marisa to go.

"I'm not ready," she whispered. "I thought I was, but I'm not."

It was Emily who comforted her.

"Don't be scared," she said.

"Who are you talking to?" her mother asked.

"Marisa."

"But Marisa's — not here."

Dead people can't see other dead people.

"She is."

But Emily can see them all.

Emily's mother wasn't going to argue. She was just so happy to have Emily back. . . .

"I'm so sorry I wasn't with you," she said. "I'm sorry I ever put you on that plane. I promise it will all be better now."

"But, Mom, you *were* on the plane with me."

Emily's mom smiled placatingly. "No, honey, I wasn't. But that's okay, since we'll —"

Suddenly, the smile fell. The words stopped.

Emily's mom covered her mouth with her hands. Her eyes grew wide. She began to shake.

"No," she said. "NO. I can't be . . ."

"Mom?"

"NO!"

"Now she knows, doesn't she?" Marisa asked nervously.

Cole nodded.

Emily's mom looked at him imploringly.

"What's going on?" she asked, her voice taut. "WHAT IS HAPPENING? I was on the plane, wasn't I? And I . . . I . . ."

She could not say the word.

Died.

"How much time do I have left?" she asked Cole. "Can you tell me how much time?"

Cole couldn't bear to say it, but he knew he had to.

"You have to say good-bye," he told her. "You have enough time to say good-bye."

"But I don't want to say good-bye! How can I say good-bye?!?"

Marisa hadn't let go of Emily's hand. She'd been listening to Cole this whole time.

"I love you, Emily," she whispered to her sister.

"Even when you were being a total pain, I loved you. I want you to remember me always, and I want you to know that you are the best sister anyone could ever have. I'm going to miss you, but part of me will always be with you. Whenever you want someone to talk to, you can always talk to me."

"I will," Emily whispered, growing tired now. "I will talk to you."

Marisa squeezed Emily's hand.

She would remember that squeeze for the rest of her life.

"It's happening," Marisa told Cole. "I can feel it. Emily's safe. She doesn't need me anymore."

"I don't want you to go," Cole whispered.

"I don't want to go, either," Marisa said. "We would've been friends, Cole. If none of this had happened, we would have been friends."

"We *are* friends," Cole insisted.

Marisa smiled under her tears. "Thanks."

Her mother was still sobbing in disbelief.

"You have to tell her to say good-bye," Marisa said. "I don't want to go alone."

Emily heard her. She turned to her mother and said, "Marisa needs you."

"Marisa?" her mother gasped.

"Yes," Emily said. "She's here. She needs you to go with her."

"But I can't leave you," Emily's mom said, clutching her hand. "I can't leave you all alone."

"I won't be alone."

Emily's mother looked deeply into her eyes. "There are so many things I have to tell you. If I let you go, you'll never know them. Don't forget your grandparents — they loved you very much. Be good to your aunt. Don't ever let anyone push you around. *Never forget you're my daughter.*"

"I won't, Mom. I won't."

They were both crying now. Cole wanted to leave them alone, but he couldn't leave while Chernenko was still by the door.

Cole watched Emily's mom and saw the change — she was suddenly filled with strength, resolve. It was the same strength and resolve that her two daughters possessed.

"I love you, Emily," she said.

"I love you, too."

Marisa looked to Cole, her expression serene.

"Good-bye, Cole," she said.

"Good-bye, Marisa," he replied, his heart breaking.

She bent over to Emily and kissed her on the forehead. "Good-bye, Shrimp," she whispered.

"Good-bye," Emily whispered.

"Remember me."

"I will."

A shudder passed through Marisa's body. "Mom!" she cried out.

Her mother looked right at her. "Marisa?"

They both hugged Emily tight and whispered last words. Cole turned away. When he turned back, they were gone.

"Good-bye," Emily whispered.

The door opened and a nurse burst into the room.

"What's going on here?" she asked angrily.

Before Detective Brown could explain, she had moved over to Emily's side.

"She's awake!" the nurse cried. "Holy God, she's awake!"

TWENTY

Cole and Detective Brown were chased out of the room by the doctors and the nurses. It was some time before they could see Emily again. They sat in the waiting room with Emily's aunt and her boyfriend.

Chernenko waited in the hall outside.

Finally, one of the doctors came back and told Emily's aunt that she could see Emily. When she came back to the waiting room, she looked overwhelmed. She walked over to Cole.

"She wants to see you now," she said.

"Let's go," Detective Brown said.

Detective Brown didn't want to burden Emily with too much at once. At the same time, the man wanted answers as quickly as possible. He brought his case file into Emily's room.

Amazingly Emily already looked a hundred percent better than she had only an hour ago. She was still hooked up to tubes and wires, but now it seemed like she was keeping them going, not vice versa.

Cole walked over to her bedside and introduced himself and Detective Brown.

"You saw them, too, didn't you?" Emily asked. "My mom . . . and Marisa."

Cole nodded.

"Thank you for helping them," she said.

Cole told her, "I liked them. They . . . your sister . . . we were sort of friends, even."

They both paused, not knowing what else to say. Cole didn't know whether to talk about the other dead people or not — was it possible that Emily could only see her relatives? Had she ever seen dead people before?

He was glad Chernenko had stayed outside.

"We have a few questions to ask you," Detective Brown said gently. "About the crash. Do you mind talking about it?"

"No." Emily seemed as brave as her mom had said.

"If at any time you want to stop, just tell me and

we'll stop." He gestured to his tape recorder. "I'm going to record what you say."

"Okay."

"Now," Detective Brown asked carefully, "what do you remember about the crash?"

Emily breathed in too deeply and had a coughing fit. Cole took a glass of water from the side table and held it to her lips. She drank gratefully.

"Thanks," she said to him. "I don't remember everything, but I remember a lot. I was in my seat. Mom and Marisa were next to me. We were in the front."

"By the cockpit?" Detective Brown asked.

"Yes, by the cockpit. I was reading my Baby-sitters Club book and a man walked past me in the aisle. He looked very angry and he was shouting things. Nobody else paid attention. I tried to ignore him. Then I saw him go near the cockpit."

"What did you do?"

"I know I was supposed to stay in my seat. But I knew I had to stop him." A tear pooled in Emily's eye and ran down her cheek. "I didn't stop him in time."

"What happened?" Detective Brown probed gently.

"I jumped up. The stewardess lady told me to get

back in my seat. She tried to stop me. But I went around her. The man was going into the cockpit. I followed him in. He was screaming so loud. *But nobody heard.* They told me to get out of the cockpit. It was too late. The man grabbed the controls. They tried to stop him. But they couldn't."

"Do you remember the man?"

"I think so."

Detective Brown reached for his case folder. Cole kept an eye on the door, waiting for Chernenko to make his move.

"I have some photos here," Detective Brown explained to Emily. "Would it be okay if I showed them to you?"

"I'm okay," Emily answered.

Detective Brown took out the photo of Chernenko that had been on all the news broadcasts. He held it up for Emily to see.

"Is this him?"

Emily paused for a moment. Cole held his breath. She shook her head slightly.

"No?"

"No."

Detective Brown wasn't deterred. He took out another photo of Chernenko.

"No," Emily said again.

Now Detective Brown was starting to get flustered. He started to pull photo after photo of Chernenko.

Emily said no to every one.

"Are you sure?" Detective Brown asked.

"I'm sure."

Detective Brown shook his head. "I don't get it," he said.

But Cole was on another thought. He remembered all of the dead people's anger — the way they tore at him, destroyed his house, struck out at the world.

"You said that nobody else saw this guy when he went into the cockpit?" he asked Emily.

Emily nodded as well as she could.

"Do you think . . . is it possible . . . that he was dead?"

Detective Brown stared at Cole, stunned. Then he turned to Emily in time to see her nod again. Remembering the words on the flight recorder, he reached into his folder and picked out a photo of the three terrorists who had hijacked Flight 165 four years ago.

The three terrorists who had died.

"That's him," Emily whispered, her eyes scared for the first time.

"Which one?" Detective Brown asked quietly.

"The middle one," Emily answered.

Cole looked down at the man in the middle of the photo. He held an assault rifle and looked commanding.

"Alexi Voltarin," Detective Brown murmured. He turned to Emily once again.

"Are you sure?" he asked her.

But both he and Cole already knew Emily was sure.

The dead terrorist had stayed around to finish what he'd started. He had probably haunted the plane for years, waiting for the right time.

If Cole hadn't seen the way dead people acted, he might not have believed it.

But he could believe it all too well, knowing what he did.

When he and Detective Brown left the room minutes later, Chernenko was nowhere to be found.

He had already moved on. Now that the true cause of the crash has been found, he no longer had to stay and clear his name.

TWENTY-ONE

"So what are you going to do about it?" Lynn Sear asked after Cole and Detective Brown had told her what had happened. They were sitting in the Sears' living room. Detective Brown had even removed his hat as a gesture to Lynn.

"I don't know what we can do," the cop answered.

"Can't we just tell the truth?" Cole asked.

Detective Brown shook his head. "It's not as easy as that. I'm going to be completely honest with you — and you might not like what I have to say. We're in a pretty bad position here. If I go to the FAA and say I have the testimony of two kids who see dead people — well, Agent McCrum will look at me with polite confusion, and Agent Masino will kick me right out of his office. And from where he sits, I can't blame him."

"Can't you have Emily talk to him?" Cole asked. "He might believe her."

"I doubt it, honey," Lynn said. "I hate to agree with your friend here, but I think he's right. If anyone ever finds out that Emily has your gift, her life will be ruined. The people who don't believe her will think she's crazy. And the people who *do* believe her will hound her for the rest of her life. She's gone through enough already — it's going to be hard enough for her to start a whole new life."

"But she's telling the truth!" Cole protested.

"I know," Lynn said. "But who does the truth help? Only Chernenko. And sometimes you have to put the living before the dead. It might be enough for him to know that we know the truth. It might be enough for him to know that the one survivor knows he's not to blame."

It was starting to make sense to Cole. He thought of the flight attendant who'd thought she was responsible for the crash because she let Emily into the cockpit. She was probably gone now, too.

"So we're not going to tell anybody?" Cole asked.

Detective Brown nodded. "This is going to be our secret. I'm going to talk to Emily and explain how things are. I also am going to talk to her about sharing the truth with her aunt. It would be great if Emily had someone around like your mom here."

Lynn looked flustered, and covered it with a joke.

"Maybe we can all form a support group," she said, trying to find a comic tone. "Mothers of children who see dead people. It'll be like the PTA."

Detective Brown was quiet for a moment. Cole realized he was thinking of his own mother.

Lynn realized it, too.

"I'm sorry," she said. "Sometimes humor is the only thing you have."

"Absolutely," Detective Brown replied. He pulled the recorder out of his jacket and removed the cassette. In front of Cole and Lynn, he pulled the tape from the cassette, making the recording meaningless.

"Nobody is ever going to know but us and Emily," he said.

"Nobody," Cole and Lynn agreed.

A few minutes later, Detective Brown said he had to go back to the hospital.

Before he left, he put a firm hand on Cole's shoulder.

"Thank you for trusting me, Cole," he said. "I'm sure we'll be in touch."

Cole didn't doubt it.

Right before dinner, Jason called. Cole was happy to hear his voice — the voice of someone who had no idea what had just happened.

"What's up?" Jason asked.

Cole didn't know where to begin, so he just said, "Not much."

"What are you up to?"

"Not much."

"I thought you said you were busy this weekend?"

Cole smiled. "It ended early."

"Wanna come to my house, then? My mom and dad say you can even sleep over."

Cole took the phone in the kitchen to ask his mom. She looked a little doubtful at first, but then he shot her his best *Please please please* look. Of course, she gave in.

"I'll be over at six," Cole told Jason. After he hung up, he went back to the kitchen to thank his mom.

"No problem," she said. He could tell something was bothering her.

"What is it?" he asked.

She looked him right in the eye. "This was a pretty bad one, wasn't it?"

"Sort of."

"Are we okay?"

Cole went over and hugged her. "Yes, we're okay," he whispered.

Luckily, Jason had enough games to take Cole's mind off of anything. Jason seemed determined to play every single one of them, and Cole wasn't about to argue.

By the time Mrs. Black told them to go to sleep, it was after eleven. Cole was totally exhausted.

Jason had erected a tent in the middle of his room — just like Cole's. He had set up two sleeping bags (and plenty of junk food) inside.

They talked for a while about school, friends, and other things. It was only when Cole's eyelids were feeling very heavy that Jason brought up the crash.

"Do you still have nightmares?" he asked.

"Yes," Cole said. "But I don't think I'm going to have any tonight."

Jason looked satisfied with that answer. "Me, neither," he said.

They fell asleep inside the tent. Cole didn't dream of the crash — instead he stayed awake, imagining Marisa and her mom in a wonderful garden. He missed Marisa like he missed Malcolm — they had both helped him through some really hard times. Now that things seemed a little better, he could think about them and wish they were still around. He wanted to tell Malcolm about everything that had happened in the past few days — with the crash, and Emily, and Detective Brown. He wanted to tell Malcolm about how close he'd come to giving up and breaking down. But Malcolm was somewhere else now. Cole didn't know where.

He hoped it was a better place.

Cole listened closely to the sound of Jason's breathing. To the sound of Jason's house — the whir of the refrigerator, the creaking of the floorboards, the slight clicking of the thermostat.

This was what normal life sounded like.

Cole would try to hold on to it for as long as he could.

Until the next dead person came around.